1/28/2012

this world we live in

SUSAN BETH PFEFFER

this world we live in

GRAPHIA

HOUGHTON MIFFLIN HARCOURT
Boston • New York

All rights reserved. Published in the United States by Graphia,
an imprint of Houghton Mifflin Harcourt Publishing Company.
Originally published in hardcover in the United States by Harcourt
Children's Books, an imprint of Houghton Mifflin Harcourt Publishing
Company, 2010.

Graphia and the Graphia logo are trademarks of Houghton Mifflin Harcourt
Publishing Company.

For information about permission to reproduce selections from this book, write to
Permissions, Houghton Mifflin Harcourt Publishing Company, 215 Park Avenue South,
New York, New York 10003.

www.hmhbooks.com

Text set in Spectrum MT

The Library of Congress has cataloged the hardcover edition as follows:
Pfeffer, Susan Beth, 1948–
This world we live in / by Susan Beth Pfeffer.
p. cm.
Summary: When the moon's gravitation pull increases, causing massive natural disasters on earth,
Miranda and her family struggle to survive in a world without cities or sunlight, and wonder if anyone
else is alive.
[1. Survival—Fiction. 2. Family life—Fiction. 3. Diaries—Fiction. 4. Science fiction—Fiction. 5. Great
Britain—History—19th century—Fiction.] I. Title.
   PZ7.P44855Ti 2010
   [Fic]—dc22
      2009026939

ISBN: 978-0-547-24804-2 hardcover
ISBN: 978-0-547-55028-2 paperback

Manufactured in the United States of America
DOM 10 9 8 7 6 5 4 3 2 1

4500285209

For Anyone Who Ever Wondered

What Happened Next

this world we live in

April

Chapter 1

April 25

I'm shivering, and I can't tell if it's because something strange is going on or because of the dream I had or just because I'm in the kitchen, away from the warmth of the woodstove. It's 1:15 AM, the electricity is on, and I'm writing in my diary for the first time in weeks.

I dreamed about Baby Rachel. I dream about her a lot, the half sister I've never met. Not that I know if Lisa had a girl or a boy. We haven't heard from Dad and Lisa since they stopped here on their way west, except for a couple of letters. Which is more than I got from anyone else who's left.

Rachel was about five in my dream, but she changes age a lot when I'm sleeping, so that wasn't disturbing. She was snuggled in bed and I was reading her a bedtime story. I remember thinking how lucky she was to have a real bedroom and not have to sleep in the sunroom with Mom and Matt and Jon the way I have for months now.

Then in the dream the lights went out. Rachel wanted to know why.

"It's because of the moon," I said.

She giggled. A real little-girl giggle. "Why would the moon make the lights go out?" she asked.

So I told her. I told her everything. I explained how in May an asteroid hit the moon and knocked it a little closer to Earth, and how the moon's gravitational pull got stronger, and everything changed as a result. There were tidal waves that washed away whole cities, and earthquakes that destroyed the highways, and volcanic eruptions that threw ash into the sky, blocking out sunlight, causing famine and epidemics. All because the moon's gravitational pull was a little bit stronger than before.

"What's sunlight?" she asked.

That was when the dream turned into a nightmare. I wanted to describe sunlight, only I couldn't remember what the sky looked like before the ash blocked everything. I couldn't remember blue sky or green grass or yellow dandelions. I remembered the words—green, yellow, blue—but you could have put a color chart in front of me, and I would have said red for blue and purple for yellow. The only color I know now is gray, the gray of ash and dirt and sadness.

It's been less than a year since everything changed, less than a year since hunger and darkness and death have become so commonplace, but I couldn't remember what life—life the way I used to know it—had been like. I couldn't remember blue.

But there was Baby Rachel, or Little Girl Rachel, in her little girl's room, asking me about how things were, and I looked at her, and she wasn't Baby Rachel anymore. She was me. Not me at five. Me the way I was a year ago, and I thought, That can't be. I'm here, on the bed, telling my half sister a bedtime story. And I got up (I think this was all the same dream, but maybe it wasn't; maybe it was two dreams and I've combined them), and I walked past a mirror. I looked to make sure I was really me, but I looked like Mrs.

Nesbitt had when I found her lying dead in her bed last fall. I was an old woman. A dead old woman.

It probably was two dreams, since I don't remember Baby Rachel after the part where I got up. Not that it matters. Nothing matters, really. What difference does it make if I can't picture blue sky anymore? I'll never see it again, anyway, or yellow dandelions or green grass. No one will, nowhere on Earth. None of us, those of us who are still lucky enough to be alive, will ever feel the warmth of the sun again. The moon's seen to that.

But horrible as the dreams were, they weren't what woke me. It was a sound.

At first I couldn't quite place it. I knew it was a sound I used to hear, but it sounded alien. Not scary, just different.

And then I figured out what the sound was. It was rain. Rain hitting against the roof of the sunroom.

The temperature's been warming lately, I guess because it's spring. But I couldn't believe it was rain, real rain, and not sleet. I tiptoed out of the sunroom and walked to the front door. All our windows are covered with plywood except for one in the sunroom, but it's nighttime and too dark to see anything anyway, unless you open the door.

It really is rain.

I don't know what it means that it's raining. There was a drought last summer and fall. We had a huge snowstorm in December and then another one later on, but it's been too cold and dry for rain.

I probably should have woken everyone up. It may never rain again. But I have so few chances to be alone. The sunroom is the only place in the house with heat, thanks to the firewood Matt and Jon spent all summer and fall chopping. We're in there together day and night.

I know I should be grateful that we have a warm place to live. I have a lot to be grateful for. We've been getting weekly food deliveries for a month now, and Mom's been letting us eat two meals a day. I'm still hungry, but nothing like I used to be. Matt's regained the strength he lost from the flu, and I think Jon's grown a little bit. Mom's gotten back to being Mom. She insists we clean the house as best we can every day and pretend to do some schoolwork. She listens to the radio every evening so we have some sense of what's happening in other places. Places I'll never get to see.

I haven't written in my diary in a month. I used to write all the time. I stopped because I felt like things were as good as they were ever going to get, that nothing was going to change again.

Only now it's raining.

Something's changed.

And I'm writing again.

April 26

I didn't tell anyone it rained last night. When you share a room with three people and a cat, anything you can keep secret feels good.

This morning I thought maybe I'd dreamed the rain, the way I dreamed Baby Rachel turning into me and me turning into Mrs. Nesbitt (dead Mrs. Nesbitt, at that), but I'm pretty sure it did rain. When I made my bedpan-emptying run, it seemed like more snow had melted.

I never thought I'd yearn for mud and slush. Then again, I never thought I'd be responsible for bedpan emptying.

I wonder if it rained where Dad, Lisa, and the baby are.

I'd rather wonder about stuff like that than wonder if they're still alive.

Sometimes I ask myself what I'd give up to see Dad again or even to know how he is. Would I give up a meal a day for the rest of my life? Would I give up electricity? Would I give up my home?

It doesn't matter. At some point the two meals a day will become one, the electricity will vanish, and we'll have to leave here just to survive.

When that happens, I know I'll never see Dad again, or Lisa, or Baby Rachel, who may not even exist. Because once we leave here, Dad will never be able to find us, just like we can't find him, or any of my friends who left here hoping things would be better someplace else.

We stayed behind. I tell myself we've made it through the worst and we can face whatever will happen next. I tell myself what Mom always says, that as long as we're alive, hope is alive.

I just wish I knew if Dad was alive also.

April 27

It rained again.

This time it rained hard for most of the afternoon.

You would have thought it was raining food and sunlight and dandelions, everyone was so excited. Even Horton tried to get out when we went to the front door to check on things. Jon shoved him back in.

"We should get pails," Mom said. "Buckets. Pans. Anything that'll hold the rainwater."

We raced around the house finding containers. We got soaking wet putting them outside, and none of them filled up all that much. When we poured the water into a couple of pots, though, it looked more impressive.

"Do you think it'll rain again?" Jon asked after we'd dried ourselves off and hung the towels on the sunroom wash line.

"It rained a couple of nights ago," I said.

Everyone stared at me. I couldn't tell if that was a good thing or not.

"The sound woke me," I said.

"You should have told us," Mom said. "We could have put pots out."

"I didn't think of it," I said. "I had a bad dream and I woke up and heard the rain falling. Or maybe I heard the rain falling and then I woke up. I don't know."

Mom sighed. It was her "Miranda is never going to grow up and be responsible and understand that when it's raining she needs to let me know so I can put pots and pans outside and catch the water and make all our lives easier" sigh.

"What?" I said. "It was raining. I didn't wake you up. It stopped raining. Now it's raining again, and for all we know it's going to rain every day for the rest of our lives and we'll float away to sea."

"What if the rain washes away the snow and then it stops raining?" Jon asked. "What would we do for water?"

"If the snow melts, the well will fill up," Mom said. "As long as the pipes don't freeze, we'll be fine."

"Running water," I said. "Now that we have electricity sometimes, it'll be a lot easier to do laundries."

"It's funny," Mom said. "The things we used to take for granted. Water. Power. Sunlight."

"We still don't have sunlight," Matt pointed out. "And we can't count on power. Or water, for that matter."

Mom looked at the pot with all the accumulated rainwater. "It's a good sign, though," she said. "A sign better things are coming."

It started raining again yesterday afternoon, and it hasn't stopped since. A heavy, steady rain.

Mom decided to celebrate by giving Jon and me pop quizzes.

Jon flunked his. Mom got all scowly.

"What difference does it make?" Jon asked. "So what if I don't learn algebra?"

"Someday schools will be open again," Mom said. "Things will be more normal. You need to do your work now for when that happens."

"That's never going to happen," Jon said. "And even if schools do open up somewhere, they're not going to open up here. There aren't enough people left."

"We don't know that," Mom said. "We don't know how many people are like us, holed up, making do until times get better."

"I bet whoever they are, they aren't studying algebra," Jon said.

I went upstairs to Mom's room to find something to read. I've read every book in my room so many times, I can open them to any page and recite it from memory.

At least it feels that way.

Mom likes biographies, which don't usually interest me, and given everything that's happened in the past year, interest me even less. Sure, Mary Queen of Scots spent most

· 7 ·

of her life in prison and then got her head chopped off, but compared to me she had it easy.

How much volcanic ash did she have to breathe every day?

One good thing about those biographies, though, is I haven't read them. Not all of them, not all the way through. And since I can't go to a bookstore or the library to get anything new to read, I went up to Mom's room to find something.

Mom expects us to keep our bedrooms as clean as possible, even though we're rarely in them. I noticed right away that there was no dust on the furniture or even on the books. I pulled one off the shelf, looked to see if I'd find it even remotely interesting, decided I wouldn't, and took another one instead.

I noticed something sticking out of the third book I looked at, a piece of paper about halfway in, and pulled it out. It was a shopping list. Mom had probably used it as a bookmark.

Milk
Romaine
OJ
WWB
Butter
Eggs
Raspberry Preserves

That was it. That was the whole list, just seven items. It took me a moment to figure out that WWB is whole-wheat bread. It's been so long since I've had any bread, let alone whole-wheat.

It's been so long since I've eaten any of those foods. So

long since I'd even thought about raspberry preserves or butter.

I can't say staring at that list (and I couldn't take my eyes off it) made me hungry, because I'm always hungry. The food we get every week is enough to keep us going, not enough to keep us full. And it sure didn't make me nostalgic. Oh, for the good old days when you could actually breathe the air and put a little raspberry preserves on your whole-wheat French toast! Mary Queen of Scots probably missed French toast, assuming it was invented by then, but not me. I'm past all that.

No, it was the romaine that got me. Seeing "romaine" in Mom's handwriting, written who knows when, made me think about who we were, who we used to be. We were a family that ate romaine. Other families ate iceberg, or Bibb, or Boston lettuce. We ate romaine. The Evans family of Howell, PA, favored romaine.

What about other people who ate romaine and raspberry preserves? Are we the only people left on Earth who did?

Somewhere there must be a place where people are eating eggs and drinking milk. I don't know where, or how they get the food, but I bet somewhere in what's left of America, there are places with food and electricity and lots of books to read.

The president had kids. The vice president had grandkids. Millionaires and senators and movie stars had families. Those kinds of people don't subsist on two cans of vegetables a day.

I wonder if they make shopping lists. I wonder if they prefer romaine.

I hate Sundays. And this one feels even worse because it's the last Sunday in April.

Mr. Danworth brings us our bags of food on Mondays, along with a little bit of news and the sense that there are people still living in Howell. But every Sunday, even though none of us says anything, we worry that he won't show up, that the food delivery will have stopped, that things will go back to where they were in the winter, with us all alone and slowly starving.

Only it would be worse now, because for a little while we've had food, so we've had reason to hope.

If I hadn't started writing in my diary again, I wouldn't realize it's the last Sunday in April. There's no reason to think things are going to change just because the calendar does, but it's one more thing to worry about. Maybe the food deliveries were going to last only through April.

I hate Sundays.

May

Chapter 2

May 1

There was no food delivery.

We spent the whole day waiting for it. Every sound we heard made one of us jump. After a while Mom gave up pretending that Jon and I were studying.

It's never light, but with it being spring, it's getting less dark later. Finally, though, we knew it was nighttime and Mr. Danworth wasn't coming.

"We're okay for a few days," Mom said. "We still have food in the pantry. A week's worth if we're careful."

I know what "careful" means. It means we eat one meal a day and Mom stops eating altogether.

"Just because we didn't get a delivery doesn't mean there isn't any food," Matt said. "Maybe Mr. Danworth can't use the snowmobile anymore. Maybe they ran out of gas. I'll go to town tomorrow and see."

"You're not going alone," Mom said. "Miranda can go with you."

"Why can't I go?" Jon whined.

"Because you flunked your algebra quiz," Mom said.-

It's funny. I've felt holed up here for so long, you'd

think I'd be excited at the thought of going someplace, any-place, even if it's just to town. But it scares me.

What if there's no one there?

May 2

Mom made Matt and me eat breakfast this morning. She said she and Jon would eat later, but we all knew that meant Jon would eat and Mom would forget to.

We decided to take our bikes, riding them when we could and pulling them along when we had to. We used to bike into town last summer, but I stopped once I started getting scared about what I might see. Then, after the bliz-zard, we couldn't bike anyway.

There was pavement for most of the trip. Some places, though, the rain and the snowmelt had left a layer of ice, and we walked and skidded there. Both of us fell more than once, but neither of us broke any bones.

That's what constitutes a good trip. No broken bones.

"City Hall may not be open," I said to Matt. "I think it's only open on Fridays."

"Then we'll go back on Friday," Matt said. "If it's closed then, we'll figure out what to do."

"We'll have to leave," I said. "Maybe we should anyway. Find a school where Jon can learn algebra."

"Mom wants us to stay for as long as possible," Matt said.

"If there's no food, we can't stay," I said.

"You're not telling me anything I don't already know," Matt said.

"I'm sorry," I said, even though I wasn't. Sometimes I think Mom and Matt make all the decisions and don't care what I think.

With the four of us cooped up in the same room to-gether day and night, I don't know when Mom and Matt have the time to whisper conspiratorially about my future, but I guess they still do. They probably talk about Jon's future in algebra while they're at it.

"I don't know if I agree with Mom," Matt said, which I knew was his way of apologizing. "But if we do decide to move, we're better off waiting until summer."

Summer used to be a time of blue and yellow and green. Now I guess it'll be less gray. It's like no broken bones. You keep your expectations low, and "horrible" is down to "merely rotten."

"Where would we go?" I asked. "Have you and Mom talked about that?"

"Pittsburgh," Matt said. "At least for a start. That seems to be the closest place we know is still functioning."

"Do you think there are places where things are actually okay?" I asked. "I know it's gray everywhere and cold, but maybe there are places with food for every-one. Running water and electricity. Furnaces. Schools and hospitals."

"And twenty-four-hour pizza delivery," Matt said. "Think big."

"I bet there are places like that," I said. "Towns set up for politicians and rich people and celebrities."

"If there are, we don't qualify," Matt said. "But we know there are people living in Pittsburgh. If we have to, we'll resettle there."

Mom gets the Pittsburgh radio station almost every night, so we hear more about it than anyplace else. Mostly they read the lists of the dead, but they also talk about food handouts and curfews and martial law.

And I know it's dumb, but we look awful. We're thin and no matter how often we wash, our faces, our hands, our clothes are gray. A whole city of people looking like us sounds like a horror movie.

"Do we have enough food now?" I asked. "If we can't get any more, and we have to move, say tomorrow, do we have enough food to get there? Pittsburgh's got to be two hundred miles away."

"Three hundred," Matt said. "But we won't have much of a choice."

Suddenly all my dreams of living someplace civilized evaporated. "I don't want us to go," I said. "We're okay where we are. At least for now. The longer we give the world time to recover, the better off things will be when we do have to go."

Matt laughed. I couldn't tell if that meant he thought it was funny I kept changing my mind or if he thought it was funny the world would ever recover.

The road cleared up pretty good after that, and we got back on our bikes and rode the rest of the way into town. We didn't see anyone, but I was prepared for that. Most people in Howell had either left early on or died during the winter.

The City Hall door was unlocked, and when we walked in, we found Mr. Danworth. I was so relieved to see him, I almost burst out crying.

"We came to see about the food," Matt said. I could tell from his shaky voice he was near tears himself. "Is there any?"

Mr. Danworth nodded. "We're not delivering anymore," he said. "You can take your regular amount home with you today."

"Do other people know?" I asked. "Or didn't you tell anybody?"

Mr. Danworth looked uncomfortable. "We were instructed not to tell," he said. "Just stop the deliveries and whoever shows up gets food."

"What about the people who can't come in?" I asked. "What if they're too weak to or it's too far away?"

"It wasn't my decision," Mr. Danworth said. "And a few folks have come in. We're keeping City Hall open all week for anyone who makes the trip. Starting next week we'll only be open on Mondays."

"How much longer will you be getting food in?" Matt asked. "Did they tell you?"

"I'll tell you what I know," Mr. Danworth replied. "A lot of the big cities—New York, Philadelphia, even Washington—they've been shut down. New York, I know, was hit hard by the waves. I guess the other cities weren't safe, either. But the cities were getting food deliveries until everybody got moved out. There was some food left over, and it's being distributed to a handful of towns. It's all connections, and we were lucky that Mayor Ford has some. His wife's cousin is married to the governor. We got our share, maybe even more.

"Only now they don't want us delivering what we get. Maybe it's to save whatever gas we have left, or maybe it's to make sure only the strong get to eat. But the letter said we could expect food for the next few weeks at least, and we'd be told when it'll stop. If anyone didn't come in for their food, we could take that amount and give it to those people who did. Next week maybe you'll get a little more than you've been used to."

"That's awful," I said. "You're going to let people die."

"If it'll make you feel any better, give them your food," Mr. Danworth said. "I don't know anyone else alive on Howell Bridge Road, but there are other places around town you could go."

"We'll take our food," Matt said. "There are four of us. We didn't all have to come in for it, did we?"

"No," Mr. Danworth said. "One representative per family. Your bags are right here."

We took them.

"I don't like this, either," Mr. Danworth said. "It gave me pleasure to see people's faces light up when I'd bring them their food. But it's the government. It makes the rules, and we have to follow them."

"We're lucky to have what we get," Matt said. "And we appreciate your keeping City Hall open this week."

"Maybe things'll get better," Mr. Danworth said. "All the rain. That's got to mean something."

"Let's hope so," Matt said. "Come on, Miranda."

I carried out two of the bags while Matt carried the others.

"People are going to die," I said as we loaded the bags onto the bikes. "Isn't there something we can do?"

Matt shook his head. "I think you're worrying about nothing," he said. "The only ones left are strong enough to get to town. The sick, the elderly, they've either moved on or died. Take Mrs. Nesbitt. She was in great health before all this, but she couldn't survive."

"So it's only people like us," I said. "Young and healthy."

"Probably," Matt said. "Survival of the fittest. And the luckiest."

It's so hard to think that, with everything terrible that's happened, we're the lucky ones.

But we have food and we have shelter and we have family. So along with no broken bones and less gray skies, I guess that means we are.

May 4

We had four hours of electricity today, smack in the middle of the afternoon. It's the longest stretch of electricity I can remember and certainly the best timed.

Mom and I threw rainwater into the washing machine and washed all the sheets, then shirts and slacks, and finally underwear. The dryer stayed on long enough to dry everything except the underwear, which we hung on the sunroom clothesline. There was a time I would have found that embarrassing, but now I'm used to it.

We're running low on laundry detergent, though. We're running low on lots of things like that: toothpaste and tissues and shampoo. Now that I know we're going to have food a little while longer, I get to worry about not enough soap.

Since the mattresses were stripped, Matt and Jon piled them up and Matt washed the sunroom floor. Then, to push my luck, I asked if we could take the plywood off the sunroom windows. Matt put it up when the temperature plummeted, and it may not be all that warm outside, but it isn't below zero all the time.

Mom thought about it and then nodded. "Go for it," she said.

Jon and I got two hammers and we pulled the nails out, and we have windows again. With the fire going, the rain in the background, and the smell of clean clothes and clean sheets, it's positively cozy.

Usually when there's electricity, Mom turns a radio on

so she can listen to the news without using up batteries (we're running low on them, too). But today she went upstairs, came down with a CD player, and put on some Simon & Garfunkel.

"I've missed music," she said.

I can't say I've missed Simon & Garfunkel, but it was nice to hear "Bridge Over Troubled Water" again. We sang it in middle school chorus about a million years ago.

When it rains, you can forget the sky is gray all the time. If you're cold, well, that's perfectly normal on a damp, dreary day. Bad weather = good mood.

Bad weather and electricity, that is.

May 5

"I've been thinking," Matt said at lunch. "About a couple of things."

I'd been thinking, too, about nail polish. But I knew better than to mention it. "What?" I asked instead.

"First of all, if we're going to stay here, Jon and I should start chopping firewood again."

"I hate the idea of the two of you out there all day, hungry, doing all that work," Mom said.

"It has to be done," Matt said. "But I think before we start on it, Jon and I should try something else."

"What?" Jon asked.

"We know we have food for a while," Matt said. "But we could certainly use more. And I can't remember the last time we had protein. The rain got me thinking. The shad run the Delaware River in spring."

"They start in April," Jon said.

"This year they might be a little late," Matt said. "But it's safe to bet the river ice has melted. I don't know if there'll be a lot of fish, but it's worth going and catching what we can."

"Could we go tomorrow?" Jon asked. "How long will we be gone?"

"Wait a second," I said. "How come I can't go, too?"

"Wait two seconds," Mom said. "I haven't agreed to any of this yet."

Matt gave Mom a look. We've been together so much the past few months, we don't have to talk anymore. We know each other's looks to perfection.

"How long would you be gone?" Mom asked.

"A week," Matt said. "Maybe less. We're about fifteen miles from the Delaware, so Jon and I should plan on a day's travel there and back. Then it would depend on how the fish are running, how long we would stay. We'll camp out, or if there are houses we can use, we'll sleep in them. Deserted motels. We'll take some food with us, but if we're lucky, we'll catch some shad first thing, and eat that until we get home."

"You'll need rods," I said. "And flies. And I still don't see why I can't go."

"You hate fishing," Jon said.

"You don't like it, either," I pointed out.

"Yeah," Jon said. "But it'll be something to do."

"We have one fishing rod in the attic," Matt said. "And Mr. Nesbitt used to fish. There's a pretty good chance I can find his rod. If not, we'll look for one in other houses around here. It shouldn't take too long to find everything we need. When people scavenged this fall, they were looking for food, not wading boots. We have sleeping bags, so that's no problem. Nobody'll mistake us for professionals, but there probably won't be much competition, either. If we can bring back a trash bag or two of shad, we could salt them and eat off them for weeks, maybe even months."

"There's so much I don't like about this," Mom said. "Including breaking into people's houses and stealing things."

"We're not stealing from anyone who's still here," Matt said. "Mom, let's say we leave at some point. Would you object if someone came in and took our firewood?"

Mom sighed. Matt grinned. Jon looked positively giddy.

"I still don't see why I can't go," I said. "I can bike fifteen miles, same as you."

"Mom shouldn't be left alone," Matt said. "And it would be easier for me to go with Jon."

I knew I wasn't going to win, and sulking and pouting would only make everybody mad at me. Which was a shame, because I used to be really good at sulking and pouting.

"I want to break into people's houses, too," I said. "I bet I could find lots of stuff we can use."

"Like what?" Jon asked in his best "I chop firewood; I bring home fish" voice.

"Stuff you're not civilized enough to care about," I said. "Toothpaste. Deodorant. Shampoo."

"You're right," Matt said. "We should all look around the houses nearby and see what we can find."

"You can't go before Tuesday," Mom said. "Monday you and Jon can go into town to get our food. That'll give both of you a sense of what it's like to travel together. What's today, anyway?"

We all counted back to Tuesday, the last day in our lives that had meaning.

"Friday," I said, counting the fastest.

"All right," Mom said. "That will give you the weekend to look for everything you need. Rods and flies and wading boots. How are we on trash bags?"

"We still have a few," Matt said. "We haven't been throwing out much garbage lately."

"Horton will be happy," I said. "The house will stink of fish."

"We'll solve that problem when we have to," Mom said. "Along with any others that come along."

May 6

I love breaking into houses. I mean, I really love it.

We each took a neighborhood. Matt started at Mrs. Nesbitt's and worked his way down Howell Bridge Road. Jon biked over to the Pine Tree section, and I went to Shirley Court.

It's easy enough to tell if a house is vacant. No smoke from the chimney, nobody home. But I knocked on doors first, pretty comfortable that no one was watching. Shirley Court has a much more suburban feeling than Howell Bridge Road, but you could tell the whole neighborhood was deserted.

When we left the house after breakfast, Matt, Jon, and I discussed the best ways of breaking in. A lot of the houses, we figured, would be unlocked, because after the house was first left empty, the scavengers would have broken in, taken all they wanted, and not bothered locking up. But if we couldn't find enough in the houses like that, we should break a window and let ourselves in.

This is the kind of discussion you have outside, where Mom can't hear you.

We each took a trash bag, which seemed optimistic to me. Then again, I expected to find some half-full detergent containers, and they're pretty bulky.

We told Mom we'd be back by 4:00, but we didn't explain to her that we'd be going separately. You can never tell what's going to set Mom off. She might have thought we'd be safer together, but then again, together we might run into a guy with a semiautomatic who'd take us all out—although my guess is the guys with the semiautomatics left a long time ago.

It's hard to say what my favorite part of breaking and entering is. I love the adrenaline rush. Will there be someone in the house? Will I get caught? I never used to shoplift, but now I understand why some kids did it. When everything else is boring, there's something to be said for risk.

But exciting as that is, it's nothing compared to finding treasures. Bottles of shampoo, one of them almost completely full. Partly used bars of soap. Lots of detergent—so much I ended up pouring it all into an almost empty 150-ounce container. Fabric softener sheets, a luxury I'd forgotten existed.

And the toothpaste! A half-used tube here, a quarter-used tube there. Two completely untouched containers of fluoride rinse. One linen closet I ransacked had a half dozen brand-new toothbrushes. We might starve to death, but at least we'll have good teeth.

Of course I checked the kitchen cabinets first, but I only found one thing there: a box of rice pilaf that had been lodged in a corner and gone undiscovered until me.

Most of my time I spent upstairs, going through bedrooms and bathrooms. It took me four houses before I remembered cosmetic bags, but once I began searching for them, I found lots of things. Travel-sized containers of shampoo and toothpaste. Hotel bars of soap, mostly untouched. Tissue packets.

I would have loved to find six-packs of toilet paper, but no such luck. Still, every house I broke into had a partly used roll in each bathroom, and I took all of them. I pulled out all the tissues from their boxes and shoved them into one of the empty cosmetic bags.

One house had a shelf filled with paperback mysteries. Another had an unused book of crossword puzzles.

Hidden in the back of one linen closet was a twelve-pack of batteries. A bottle of aspirin sat waiting for me in a medicine cabinet. There were two cans of shaving cream I took for Matt.

So much stuff. It's amazing how much stuff people used to have.

After you've looted strangers' medicine cabinets, you don't feel much guilt when you go through their chests of drawers. I only took socks. I could have taken underwear, but the idea of wearing someone else's disgusted me. Socks, though, were a whole other matter. If nothing else, Matt and Jon were going to need a lot of them.

The Shirley Court people didn't seem to be too outdoorsy. No rods or reels or wading boots. I found a couple of ski masks, though, so I threw them in for Matt and Jon to use if they slept outdoors.

Every house I went into had a bucket, and I took a couple of them and put one on each handlebar. I filled them with the smaller things, figuring after we emptied them, we could use them to hold rainwater.

I know I found more stuff, but it's hard to remember. Every thing was a treasure waiting to be discovered.

There is nothing more beautiful than half a roll of toilet paper.

The best thing about my brand-new career as a burglar was being alone. For eight glorious hours I spoke to no one. I bumped into no one. I looked at no one. And no one spoke to me or bumped into me or looked at me.

I couldn't wait to show everybody all my loot. It was like trick-or-treating only a thousand times better. Even so, there was a part of me that was sad at the thought of giving up the quiet, unshared space.

But after eight hours I was cold, hungry, and tired. I made sure everything was securely in place and began the bike ride home.

Matt, Jon, and I had agreed to meet by the mailbox so Mom would think we'd stayed together. Matt was already there when I got back, and Jon showed up a couple of minutes later. All our bikes were loaded.

Mom tried to look disapproving, but I could see her eyes light up as we brought in our loot. After a while she got into the whole Christmasy feel.

"My brand of shampoo," she said. "Oh, and look at this. I haven't had a crossword puzzle to do in months!"

Of course we oohed and aahed over the rods and reels and flies and nets and wading boots and salt containers. Matt had also found an unopened bag of cat food for Horton and a cordless power saw that still had some power to it.

Neither one of them had thought to take the toilet paper or soap or any of the useful stuff I'd located. But I can always go back to the houses they went through.

As far as I was concerned, though, Jon found the absolute best thing. He was positively giddy when he handed a box to me. "I tried two of them," he said. "They both worked, so I bet they all do."

It wasn't a big box, but I was so excited about what I'd find, my hands shook as I opened it. In the box were twenty-four flashlight pens, all neatly inscribed "Walter's Realty Your Home Is Our Business."

I flicked one on and sure enough it worked.

"Now you can write in your journal without using a flashlight," Jon said.

I could have kissed him. In fact, I'm writing this entry after everyone else has gone to sleep, thanks to Walter's Realty. If I ever buy a house, I'll give them my business.

May 7

Mom wouldn't let us go through any more houses. "You've found enough," she said. "Stealing isn't a game."

"We're not stealing," Matt said.

"Taking things without permission," Mom said. "It's as good as stealing."

But I didn't notice her hesitating to do one of the crossword puzzles.

May 8

Matt and Jon went to town to pick up our food, and I was too jumpy to stay in the house.

"I'm going to Mrs. Nesbitt's," I said, and I was pleased Mom didn't make a fuss about stealing.

The first thing I located was a manual can opener, for Matt and Jon. None of us had thought to pick one up on Saturday. I never thought of Mrs. Nesbitt as one to travel, but sure enough, she had a cosmetic bag hidden away, with a tissue packet, a little bar of soap, and three packets of hand sanitizer. She'd left a quarter roll of toilet paper as well.

But the most interesting thing I found was a small electric heater. By the time she'd died, electricity was a thing of the past, so no one had bothered taking it.

But now, at least sometimes, we have electricity. I lugged the heater back to the house, along with whatever else I could find.

"We can use it in the kitchen," I told Mom. "Or turn it on anyplace whenever we have power."

"That's a good idea," Mom said. "We could put it in the sunroom and cut down on the firewood."

Of course when you want electricity is exactly when you don't get it. We haven't had any since those fabulous four hours a few days ago.

Mom and I then had a lengthy discussion about the causes of World War One so she could feel like we got something done. It seems like a pretty dumb war to me, but most wars seem pretty dumb to me, given how things worked out.

She had just finished telling me how the Russian royal family had all been murdered but some people thought Anastasia had survived, when Matt and Jon returned. They brought the same four bags, but there was more food in each. I knew I should feel bad about that, but I couldn't make myself.

If Mom noticed the extra two cans in each bag, she didn't say so. Instead she asked how the roads were.

"A lot better than last week," Matt said. "Almost no ice."

"We biked the whole way," Jon said. "I bet we won't have any problems getting to the river."

"All right," Mom said. "You can leave tomorrow

morning after breakfast. But no traveling after dark, and I'll expect you home by Friday."

"Saturday," Matt said. "That way we'll have three days if the fishing is good. We'll leave first thing Saturday morning."

"Saturday, then," Mom said. "Before then if there aren't any fish. Or if either one of you doesn't feel well. No heroics. And no traveling separately. If one of you leaves, you both leave. Is that clearly understood?"

"Clearly," Matt said, but he was grinning, and Jon could hardly keep still, he was so excited.

I don't blame them. If I got to go away for five whole days, I'd be landing triple axels on the living room floor.

Chapter 3

May 9

Mom made Matt and Jon eat an extra can of spinach for breakfast, and then we helped them load the bikes.

Matt remembered a folding grocery cart in Mrs. Nesbitt's cellar, so he ran over there and brought it back. He rigged it to the back of his bike to hold the fishing equipment and the sleeping bags. They both wore their backpacks, which Mom had filled with food and bottles of rainwater.

"We'll bring back trash bags full of shad," Matt promised us. "Everything's going to be better once we get back with food."

"Wear your face masks," Mom said. "And boil your drinking water. Matt, you have to be really careful."

"We will be, I promise," he said. He and Jon kissed Mom good-bye, and then Matt bent over and gave me a good-bye kiss, too.

I didn't like that. It felt too final.

We walked out with them and watched as they began their ride down Howell Bridge Road. The air is so bad you can't see too far ahead of you, but I bet they tore off their face masks a half mile down the road.

I was reading <u>Romeo and Juliet</u> (Mom figures it must be in the curriculum somewhere) and Mom was working on one of her illicit crossword puzzles when the electricity came on. We jumped into action. We put all our pots and pans in the dishwasher, threw in detergent and buckets of rainwater, and hoped for the best.

"I had a thought," Mom said, which always means More Work for Miranda. "If we could find another electric heater, we could put one in the kitchen and one in the dining room."

"The firewood's in the dining room," I said. "Besides, why would we want to eat in there?"

"We wouldn't," Mom said. "But if we stored the firewood in the pantry and had heaters for the kitchen and dining room, then Matt and Jon could share one room and you and I the other. Both rooms have windows that face the sunroom, from when it was the back porch, so they get a little bit of heat from the woodstove. Between that and the heaters and our sleeping bags, we would be warm enough."

"We'd need someone to check on the woodstove during the night," I said. "Maybe we should keep one mattress in the sunroom, and we could take turns sleeping in here." I pictured that, sleeping alone in the kitchen. Even sleeping alone in the sunroom, waking up every few hours to put in another log, sounded like heaven.

Mom and I emptied out the pantry (which didn't take very long, even with the extra food we got yesterday) and carried in all the remaining firewood. The dishwasher kept churning, and naturally we did some laundry at the same time.

Mom washed the kitchen floor while I swept every piece of bark and leftover twig from the dining room. The electricity held out long enough for us to vacuum.

"Should we move the mattresses in?" I asked once the dining room met with Mom's approval.

"Not yet," she said. "All this is dependent on having electricity fairly regularly, especially at night. That may never happen."

Great. I exhausted myself lugging firewood for a fantasy.

Mom burst out laughing when she saw me scowl. "Things will get better," she said. "I promise."

I wanted to ask how. Did she mean we'd get electricity regularly, or the sun would start shining again and we could have a vegetable garden, or Matt and Jon would come back with enough fish to last us a lifetime, or we'd move someplace with food and running water and junior proms? Senior proms, I guess, since I'd be a senior by the time there was a prom. Assuming I ever finish reading <u>Romeo and Juliet</u>.

But I didn't ask. Instead I put the second load of laundry into the dryer, throwing in one fabric softener sheet. Horton, who'd run upstairs at the sound of the vacuum cleaner, came back down and sat on my lap while I pretended to read Shakespeare by lamplight, all the while thinking about food and water, blue skies and proms.

May 10

I don't know if Horton doesn't like the food Matt found for him, or if he's holding out for the shad Matt and Jon say they'll be bringing back, or if he just misses Jon. But he hardly ate a thing.

Mom says when he's hungry he'll eat.

We'd almost run out of cat food before Matt brought home that bag, and I'd been worrying about what would happen when we did. In the olden days people fed their cats table scraps or the cats found some mice to nosh on.

But Horton would have no interest in leftover canned peas, assuming we had any left over, which we don't. And with the cold and the drought and the snow and the ice and the complete lack of sunlight, the mice have all died out.

I was six when Dad brought Horton home. Horton seemed to think Jonny was a kitten, too, because the two of them played together all the time. Horton became more Jonny's cat than anyone else's, but we all love him, and I hate the thought of life without him. He's eleven now, and he doesn't do much more than sleep and eat and sit on our laps, but he's still the blue and green and yellow in our lives.

I hope he develops a taste for his new cat food. I hope we can find some more for him or there's enough shad to go around.

May 11

I told Mom I was going to bike up and down Howell Bridge Road, stopping at the houses to look for space heaters. If I found any, I'd figure out some way of dragging them home.

"You can't go by yourself," Mom said. "It's too dangerous."

Sometimes I'm so stupid I amaze even myself. "I went all through Shirley Court by myself," I said.

"When did you do that?" Mom asked.

Then I won the Olympic Gold Medal in stupid. "On Saturday," I said. "That's where I found all my stuff."

"I thought you all went looking together," Mom said.

"We started out together," I said. "But we split up right away."

"You mean you lied to me?" Mom asked.

I knew that "you" was directed right at me. Matt didn't lie. Jon didn't lie. Only Miranda lied.

"We didn't lie," I said. "Besides, it was Matt's idea."

"I don't care whose idea it was!" Mom yelled. "It was unsafe and you knew it, and that's why you lied to me."

"I don't believe this," I said. "Matt and Jon can go anywhere they want. We don't know if we'll ever see them again, and you're mad at me for going to Shirley Court by myself?"

It's been months since Mom and I had had a real battle, and we were overdue. She screamed, "Insensitive! Uncaring!" and I screamed, "Overbearing! Playing favorites!"

Right after I shouted, "I never want to see you again!" I ran out, got my bike, and began pedaling as fast as I could. I didn't care where I ended up or even that I'd been too angry to put on my coat and it was too cold to be outside without one. I wanted to escape, the way Matt and Jon had.

I started by going down Howell Bridge Road, but I knew I didn't want to end up in town. So after a couple of miles, I turned on to Bainbridge Avenue, and then I turned again and again and again. I avoided streets I knew, because every one had a memory and I didn't dare face my memories.

I must have biked for an hour before I acknowledged I had no idea where I was and very little sense of how to get home.

I thought, Of all the stupid things I've ever done, this is the stupidest, because I could die here and no one will ever know what became of me.

That was when I totally lost it. It's been hard to cry in the sunroom, because we're together all the time, and tears are better if you shed them alone. But I've never been as alone as I was that moment, sweating and shivering and hungry and lost. First one tear trickled down and then another, and then I sobbed six months' worth of sorrow and anger and fear.

I could have cried forever, except I didn't have any tissues on me, and the only thing I had to blow my nose into was my sweatshirt. Which made me sweating and shivering and hungry and lost and really disgusting. Then I started laughing, so for a while I was laughing and crying, and then I just laughed, and then I just shook. After a few minutes of that I thought I'd be okay, but before I knew it I was sobbing again.

I told myself Mom wasn't shedding any tears over me, but I knew she was. It was like that scene in <u>The Wizard of Oz</u> where Dorothy looks in the crystal ball and sees Auntie Em crying out for her. I knew Mom was crying. She was crying because she's worried sick about Matt and Jon and now she was worried about me. Only that made me cry even harder, because I was worried about Matt and Jon, too, and I was probably a lot more worried about me than Mom was. She thought I was breaking into houses on Howell Bridge Road like a sane, disobedient daughter. I knew I was crazy and lost and cold and scared.

I knew I couldn't stay there forever, so once I'd stopped shaking from the hysteria and resumed shaking from the cold, I got back on my bike and let my legs direct me. I favored right turns, but for the longest time I was in countryside, with nothing but unoccupied farms around.

Then, because right turns weren't doing much for me, I made a left. I biked maybe a half a mile down the road, and in the distance I could see a mound of some sort.

At least it was something to look at. I biked toward it. When I got close enough that the dust in the air didn't block my view, I could see it was a mound of bodies.

I got off my bike in time to throw up. Part of me said to get back on and ride in the opposite direction, but I couldn't help looking.

The pile was about six bodies high, and it was pyramid shaped, more bodies on the bottom than the top. It wasn't neatly formed, though, and there was more snow on some places than others, so it looked kind of lumpy. The cold had preserved things, and I could see hands and feet toward the bottom of the pile and heads sticking out higher up.

People have been dying around here since the summer, but before things got too bad, the bodies were buried. There were cremations, too, although maybe they were funeral pyres. You don't ask about things like that. Not unless you absolutely have to.

But when the sun disappeared and the weather turned cold, more and more people died. Starvation, sickness, suicide. More bodies than people knew what to do with.

I thought, What if Mrs. Nesbitt is in the pile? I've known so many people who have died, but she was the only one I thought of then. Mrs. Nesbitt could be in a mound of snow-covered bodies in a field somewhere near town, and if Mom ever found that out, it would kill her. She was more than just a neighbor. She was family.

I told myself not to look but of course I did. It was hard to make out faces, between the snow and the distance, since the top of the pile was taller than me. And I didn't see Mrs.

Nesbitt, who most likely was cremated, since she'd died fairly early on. But I did see Mrs. Sanchez, my high school principal, and Michelle Webster, who I'd known since fifth grade, and the Beasley boys, two old guys without many teeth who used to sit in front of the hardware store, good weather or bad, and chatter in secret code to each other. They were descended from Jedediah Howell, the same as Mom. The same as me.

I thought I should say a prayer over these people, show them respect for the lives they led, the people they were. I don't know a lot of prayers, and the only phrase that came right to me was "deliver us from evil," which didn't seem appropriate. So I said, "I'm sorry," out loud, and then I said, "I'm sorry," again.

It could have been us. It should have been us. We have no more right to be alive on May 11th than any of them. Why should I be alive and Michelle Webster dead? She did better in school than me. She had more friends. Yet, there I was standing by her dead body.

Deliver us from evil. Deliver us to evil is more like it.

I got on my bike, pedaled as fast as I could, and discovered I was on the back road to the high school. From there I made my way back to town, back to Howell Bridge Road, back to my home, back to the sunroom.

Mom opened the door for me. I thought she'd be loving and comforting when I got in, but she wasn't.

"You came back," she said. "I wasn't sure you would."

"I had nowhere else to go," I said, walking toward the fire, desperately needing its warmth to heal me.

"The boys," she said. "Will they be coming back?"

"How can they?" I asked. "They're dead. Everybody's dead."

Mom turned white, and for a moment I thought she was going to collapse. "Matt and Jon are dead?" she screamed.

"No!" I cried. "Not Matt and Jon!" I pictured them on the mound, all of us on the mound, and I made a sound I can't even describe. It came from deep within me, the place where I hide all my rage and grief, a sound no one should ever have to hear.

"Miranda," Mom said, and she grabbed me and was shaking me. "Miranda, how did you find out? Did someone tell you?"

"I saw them!" I cried. "Oh, Mom, it was horrible. It was the worst thing I've ever seen."

"Where?" she said. "Can you take me to them? Now. We have to go now."

"All right," I said. "But you don't have to go there, Mom. I didn't see Mrs. Nesbitt. I'm sure she wasn't there."

"Mrs. Nesbitt?" Mom said. "Why would she be at the river?"

"I didn't go to the river," I said. "Is that where Matt and Jon . . ." I couldn't even finish the sentence.

Mom took a deep breath. "Matt and Jon," she said. "Are they coming back?"

"How can they come back?" I asked. "You just said they . . ." I still couldn't say it.

"I didn't," she said. "I thought you did."

"Did what?" I asked. "Said what? I came in here, and you said Matt and Jon weren't coming back."

"Tell me everything you know about Matt and Jon," she said. "Don't leave anything out."

"They left on Tuesday," I said. "They went to the Delaware River to catch shad. They're supposed to come back on Saturday. That's all I know. What do you know?"

"Exactly the same thing," Mom said. "Oh, Miranda. You gave me the scare of my life."

I stared at her, and we burst out laughing. It's funny: Horton slept through all the hysterics, but as soon as he heard us laughing (and I have to admit, our laughter was pretty hysterical), he got up and walked out of the room. Which made us laugh even more.

"What about Mrs. Nesbitt?" Mom asked. "What were you talking about, Miranda?"

I thought about Mom, how terrified she must have been that she might never see any of us again. I thought about all the people she's lost this past year.

"Nothing," I said. "I saw a field with a lot of fresh graves. The Beasley boys were there. That's who I meant when I said the boys were there. But Mrs. Nesbitt probably isn't. I hope not anyway."

Mom nodded. "There must be graves like that all over," she said. "All over the world. Come on, Miranda. Change into something warmer, and I'll make you some soup."

I did as she said. I even ate the soup. But I saw what I saw, and I know—with a cold, cruel certainty—that someday, somewhere, we'll be part of a mountain of bodies reaching up toward the sunless sky.

Chapter 4

May 12

"Matt and Jon will be home tomorrow," Mom said, as though saying it often enough would guarantee it would actually happen. "And we're going to need a place to store the fish."

"You really think they'll have that many?" I asked. My fantasies, when I've allowed myself any, are shad poached in white wine, a stuffed baked potato, and sautéed green beans. With a salad beforehand and chocolate mousse for dessert. And a hot fudge sundae.

"Let's hope so," Mom said. "I hate to think they're spending all their time in the cold not catching anything."

"Except cold," I said, which Mom might have thought was clever a year or so ago.

A year ago. May 18th is the anniversary of when the asteroid hit the moon. May 12th a year ago, I had no idea of how my life, how everyone's life, was about to change. A year ago my biggest problem . . . Well, a year ago I didn't have any problems. Maybe I thought I did but I didn't.

"I think the cellar would be best," Mom said. "It should be cool enough, at least until we salt the fish."

I don't like cellars. I don't like ours and I don't like Mrs.

Nesbitt's. Friends of mine had basements that were converted into family rooms or used for storage, but we have an old-fashioned dirt cellar. Toadstools grew there in the summer, but Mom was afraid they were poisonous, so we never ate them.

Mushrooms. I added them to my imaginary shad dinner. Feeling virtuous, I also added a chocolate peanut butter pie.

Mom grabbed our biggest flashlight and opened the cellar door. I followed her, to prove what a good daughter I am. After yesterday she still needed some convincing.

"Oh no," she said, shining the light onto the floor. Not that you could see the floor. The reflection of the light shone right back at us. The cellar was completely flooded.

"I guess we'll have to find someplace else for the shad," I said, unconvinced there'd be enough to worry about. "Maybe the garage?"

"The shad's not the problem," Mom said, which could have fooled me, since the shad had been the problem thirty seconds earlier. "We've got to clear the cellar out. We can't let it stay flooded."

"I guess the sump pump stopped working," I said. "All the snow melting and the rain and not enough electricity. Why can't the cellar stay flooded? At least until Matt and Jon get home?"

"Don't you think they've done enough for us?" Mom asked.

Actually I didn't. As far as I was concerned, they were having a wonderful adventure, away from home, away from Mom and the sunroom and mounds of bodies.

"Mom," I said, trying to sound mature and reasonable and not like a whining crybaby. "That's an awful lot of water for us to mop."

"We'll use the pails you brought home," Mom said, because sure, it was fine for me to break into people's houses just as long as I stole pails and crossword puzzle books. She walked down a few steps, then turned to me and said, "Get the folding yardstick. It's in the hardware drawer in the kitchen."

I found the yardstick and brought it to her. Mom climbed down the rest of the stairs and stuck the yardstick into the water. "Six inches," she said. "The water is six inches deep."

"We can't clean up all that water ourselves," I said.

"Why not?" Mom said. "Do you have anything better to do?"

Suddenly <u>Romeo and Juliet</u> seemed very appealing. "I'll get the pails," I said, "but I don't know how we're going to do this."

"Me either," Mom said. "Bring all the pails and that big pot we used to make soup in. Oh, and the mop. We'll need it eventually."

"How about boots?" I asked.

"Absolutely," Mom said. "And another flashlight we can leave on the steps."

So I searched the house for anything that could hold water and anything that could keep it off us.

"I've done this before," Mom said when I returned to her loaded with everything I could find. "Once when the sump pump stopped and another time when the water heater burst. A little water never hurt anyone, but it's not a good idea to let the cellar stay like this."

"How are we going to empty the pails?" I asked.

Mom paused for a moment. "It is going to take forever, isn't it?" she said. "I'll fill the pails and you can empty them outside. Tell you what. Open the kitchen window and lift the screen up and throw the water out. It's not the best method, but it'll save us time."

"We'll be better off with six containers," I said. "You can fill four while I throw out two."

"Good thinking," Mom said. "Get the biggest pots you can find."

So I did. And while I was looking for them, Mom put on her boots and started filling the pails. By the time I put on my boots and walked down the stairs, Mom had all three pails and the soup pot pretty much full. I took two pails, carried them from the cellar through the kitchen, and flung the water out. As I walked downstairs, I thought that this was the stupidest thing I'd done in a year, maybe in my entire life.

On the other hand, it kept Mom from staring at the door, willing Matt and Jon to come home. And it was a distraction from thinking about piles of dead bodies.

It didn't take more than a half dozen trips before my legs and back began aching. And I knew, after a half dozen trips, that if we'd stuck the yardstick back in the water, it would still register six inches.

But Mom kept at it, and her body had to be aching every bit as much as mine, from bending with the pot, filling it with water, and dumping the water into a pail.

We worked silently for a half hour, the only sounds the water sploshing around and my footsteps up and down the cellar stairs. I thought about saying how ridiculous this all was, but I knew better than that. I went for the lighthearted approach instead.

"It's a shame we can't let the water freeze," I said. "I could have an indoor skating rink."

Mom stood upright and stretched. "Do you miss skating?" she asked.

Compared to what? I thought. Food? Friends? Dad? But all I said was "A little bit. I liked skating on the pond this winter."

"I used to love to watch you skate," Mom said. "Don't tell Matt or Jon, because I enjoyed their track meets and baseball games, but I liked going to your skating competitions the most. It broke my heart when you had to give it up."

"Mine, too," I said.

"Sometimes I think of all the things we had and lost before," Mom said. "Your skating. Lucky, our cat before Horton. Even my parents, dying when I was so young. Maybe we lost the things we loved then so we could survive losing everything else."

"We haven't lost everything else," I said, taking the pails from her. "We still have each other and the house and Horton." And a flooded cellar and a backache.

"Isn't there some kind of Greek myth about this?" I asked on one of my return trips. "Some guy who has to empty out the ocean with a spoon and by the time he finishes, it rains for forty days and nights?"

"If there isn't, there should be," Mom said. "How long have we been at it?"

"Too long," I said, and checked my watch. "More than an hour."

Mom stretched again. "I was in labor fourteen hours with Matt," she said. "That was worse."

I thought about how unlikely it was I would ever meet any guy, fall in love, get married, have babies. Especially since I was going to spend the rest of my life in the cellar, where, in the not too distant future, I'd turn into a toad-stool. I hoped I'd be the poisonous variety.

I don't know how much longer we were working before I had my realization: Mom knew how impossible this job was and she didn't care. It was a convenient excuse to keep me from going out and looting. The only fun I'd had in months and she was determined to prevent me from doing it, even if it meant locking me in a cellar and making me empty pail after pail of water.

Okay, I wasn't locked in. And Mom was working as hard as, if not harder than, I was. But it still was an awfully convenient excuse to keep me where she could see me.

Given that I'd run away like a seven-year-old the day before, she might have had a point. But I really was capable of biking around town and looking for space heaters, boxes of rice pilaf, and half-used rolls of toilet paper.

Matt and Jon got to be out of her sight for five days. I was out for five hours, and it was down to the cellar for me.

It's funny. I'm writing all this down because I felt it, and even though I know it was immature for me to feel that way, I'm not sure I wasn't right. Maybe not 100 percent right but at least partway. If it hadn't been the cellar, Mom would have found some other job in the house for me. She wanted me where she could see me, and the cellar provided her with a great excuse to keep me by her side.

All of which, of course, put me in an even worse mood. But I kept taking the pails from her and carrying the water upstairs and flinging it out the window, because I'd done my seven-year-old running-away bit yesterday and all it had gotten me was a mound of dead bodies I'll see until the day I'm part of it.

After a while, though, I had to take a break. "I'm taking a few minutes off," I told Mom. "I'm going to check up on Horton. And I'll clean the ash out from the woodstove."

"I'll stay down here," Mom said. "If I leave, I'll never come back."

That seemed like an excellent reason to leave, but when Mom's like that, you don't try to fight. I took the pails, emptied them, tossed them back to Mom, and looked in on Horton. Or more accurately, his food bowl. He'd eaten a little since last night, but not as much as I would have liked.

I cleaned his litter while I was at it and then the woodstove. Those were Jon's jobs ordinarily. The ash pile had gotten a lot of snow mixed in over the months, and now that the snow was pretty much melted, the ash had turned into a large messy glop. It was probably killing all the plants around it, except of course there's no sunlight anymore, so the plants were dead anyway.

I stood there for a moment, thinking about the ash and the sun and death, then trudged back to the house, got to the cellar door, sighed heavily so Mom could understand what a martyr I was, and walked down the stairs, expecting to see Mom surrounded by full pails of water for me to ditch.

Only Mom wasn't surrounded by anything. She was lying, face down, in the water.

I first thought, She's dead. She's dead and I killed her. And for a second I was frozen with terror and guilt. She must have fainted, I thought, and fallen face down in the water. You can drown in six inches just as easily as six feet.

They say in the moment before you die, your whole life

passes in front of you. All I know is Mom's whole life passed in front of me. All her hopes. All her fears. All her anger.

The moment passed as quickly as it had arrived, and I raced down the stairs to get to her. I'm a swimmer. I've taken lifesaving courses. I hadn't dawdled that long outside, and for all I knew, Mom had collapsed five seconds before I found her.

I yanked her up out of the water and gave her mouth-to-mouth until she began breathing on her own.

When I was sure she was alive and conscious, I pulled her up the stairs into the kitchen and then into the sunroom. She was still coughing, but she hadn't died some stupid, meaningless death.

I wanted to yell at her, to tell her never to do anything like that again, but instead I ran for towels. She was shaking too hard to undress herself, so I took her clothes off. She's so thin. She's eaten less than any of us so we can all have a little bit more.

I dried her off, but she was still shaking, so I heated some water on the woodstove and sponge-bathed her, then dried her off again. I found clean clothes for her to put on, extra socks and a coat, even though the sunroom is pretty warm. I wrapped a blanket around her, then used up one of our last tea bags and made her a cup to sip. Horton jumped on her lap, and she stroked him until they were both comforted.

"I don't know what happened," she said. "I was all right, waiting for you before I began working again, and then I must have passed out."

"It doesn't matter," I said. "I found you. You're fine."

"Would I have died?" she asked. "Could I have really died that way? After all we've been through, could that have happened?"

I knew she was asking herself those questions, so I didn't say anything. She'd stopped shaking, and for me that was enough.

Neither one of us mentioned going back to the cellar. Let the house sink into the earth. Mom's avoided the mound of death for one more day, and that's all that matters.

Chapter 5

May 13

Mom was a nervous wreck waiting for Matt and Jon to return. She kept looking at her watch like they were late for curfew.

I was anxious for them to get back, too. The past few days without them hadn't been particularly pleasant.

At least Mom didn't make us go back into the cellar. I was afraid she would, to give us something to do while we waited. But instead she leafed through one of the mysteries I'd taken without permission. It's Saturday, so I don't have to do schoolwork, but I pretended to read my history textbook anyway.

We both heard them, the sounds of their bikes, the sounds of their laughter, at about the same time. I got to the door first, opened it, and waited for them to cross the threshold so I could hug them and keep them from ever leaving again.

But when they did cross the threshold everything was different. Forever different.

There was Jon, holding on to a trash bag filled with fish. There was Matt, looking even happier than the day he got into Cornell. And there, clinging to Matt's arm, was a girl.

"This is Syl," Matt said. "My wife." He grinned. "I love the sound of that," he said. "Syl. My wife."

"Your wife," Mom said, and it was obvious she didn't love the sound of that. "Matt, Jon, come in. Miranda, take that bag and put it in the garage. We'll deal with it later."

"There's another bag," Jon said. "I'll go with you, Miranda."

"Great," I said, taking it from him and walking to the bike. Jon got the second bag, as full as the first, and we began the walk to the garage.

"Wife?" I whispered. "What happened? Who is she?"

"We were at this motel," Jon said, like he was bursting to tell me. "It was the second night. There are empty motels all over. You find a room and take it. You know how there's a door to another room right in yours? We could hear a man screaming at a girl in the room next door. It sounded like he was hitting her. Matt broke the door down, and he ran in there and grabbed her and told the guy to keep his hands off her if he knew what was good for him."

"Matt did that?" I asked. "And the girl was Syl?"

Jon nodded. "He brought her back into our room, and we got our stuff and went upstairs to a different room. The guy could have tried to find us, but he acted like he didn't care when we took Syl away. He said she was all ours, as far as he was concerned. He meant it, too, because the next day, he was at the river fishing, and he said hi to us like we were old friends. Syl didn't seem scared of him, but I don't think she scares easy. The next night, though, we stayed at a different motel."

He paused for a moment. "Syl said I should take a room to myself, that she and Matt could share. That was Thursday night. Yesterday we went back to the river, and Matt said he and Syl had exchanged vows and in the eyes of God they were married. There was a guy at the river whose wife had died months ago, and he took off his wedding ring and gave it to Matt to put on Syl's finger. It's too big for her and it keeps falling off."

"Mom is going to kill him," I said.

Jon nodded. "Matt won't care," he said. "He's crazy. Everybody's crazy, Miranda. It was great at the river because there were people there, and we talked about stuff, like how NASA must be working on ways of growing plants without sunlight so we'll all have food again, but you could tell everybody was crazy. Anytime someone caught a fish, there'd be singing and dancing like they'd won the lottery."

"Do you like her?" I asked.

"I think so," Jon said. "She talks to me like she's interested. She talks to everybody that way. On the ride home she and I talked. She and Matt were on his bike, and I was on mine, and Matt kept whistling and singing, but Syl and I talked. I told her about you and Mom and Dad and Lisa and Horton. We talked about baseball, too, but she doesn't know anything about it."

I knew we had to get back into the house, but I had so many more questions. "Where's she from?" I asked. "Did she tell you anything?"

Jon shook his head. "I did most of the talking," he said. "But she must have told Matt. He wouldn't have married her if he didn't know more about her."

I had a feeling there was a difference between exchanging vows in a motel room and actually being married, but Matt apparently didn't care. "We'd better get inside," I whispered. "Before Mom divorces them."

Jon laughed nervously. I guess he'd been thinking the same thing since yesterday morning.

"You're back," Mom said as Jon and I walked in. "We were just chatting. Syl's such an interesting name. Is it short for something?"

"It wasn't the name I was born with," Syl said. "It's for Sylvia Plath, the poet."

"I know who Sylvia Plath is," Mom said.

I looked at Syl then, and I could understand why Matt had fallen in love. She's gorgeous. We're all thin now, but she looks intentionally thin, model thin. It was like the entire world came to an end just so you could really notice her cheekbones. And her hair. None of us have much hair, since we cut it months ago when it got hard to wash. But Syl's hair is a braid to her waist. And even though the ash in the water makes everything look dingy, somehow her hair and clothes look clean. Or at least cleaner than I'm used to.

"Syl's great," Jon said. "She cleaned the fish." He bent over and stroked Horton, who was the only happy one in the room. It probably helped that Jon reeked of fish.

"That was very nice of you, Syl," Mom said. "I doubt Miranda was looking forward to that."

I hadn't given cleaning fish any thought whatsoever. "The cellar's flooded," I said, to hold up my end of the conversation. "Mom and I tried to dry it out yesterday, but it was too much for us."

No one else seemed interested. "I thought I'd take the sofa-bed mattress," Matt said. "And move it into my room for Syl and me. If we push the furniture around, the mattress should fit on the floor."

"I found an electric space heater," I said. "You could keep it on, and whenever there's electricity, it'll warm the room up."

"That would be great," Matt said. "Thank you, Miranda."

"We moved the firewood into the pantry," I said. "We were thinking about using the dining room and the kitchen as bedrooms. Maybe you'd prefer that."

"No, we'll have more privacy in my room," Matt said.

Mom looked like a volcano waiting to erupt. "Saying a few words doesn't make you married," she said.

"Of course it does," Matt said. "That's what marriage vows have always been, saying a few words. Yeah, Syl and I didn't have a minister or bridesmaids or rice, but that doesn't make us any less married. Not in this world, Mom. No one has bridesmaids in this world."

"They could go to City Hall on Monday, Mom," Jon said. "If the mayor's there, he could marry them."

"Jon, stay out of this," Mom said. "You, too, Miranda."

It's kind of hard to stay out of things when we're all living in the same room. "Come on, Jon," I said. "Let's get Matt's room ready for them."

"Stay where you are!" Mom said. "Matt, you and Jon will sleep in the dining room. Miranda, Syl, and I will share the sunroom."

"No," Matt said. "Syl isn't some stray cat I picked up on the road. We're married and we intend to stay that way for the rest of our lives. If you can't accept that, we'll leave."

I thought about how I'd run away a couple of days

before, how easy it is to get lost forever, how easy it is to end up just another dead body on a mound. "Don't go," I said. "Mom doesn't want you to go. You know that, Matt."

Mom inhaled, like she was shoving the lava back into place. "Syl," she said. "Please understand this isn't about you. I'm sure you're very nice. If Matt had brought you home under different circumstances, ordinary circumstances, I'd be delighted."

"These are ordinary circumstances," Matt said. "And they have been for a year now. Mom, Syl's the best thing that's ever happened to me. I feel alive now. I don't know if I'll still be alive six months from now. But whatever time I have, I'm going to spend it with her."

"And you, Syl," Mom said. "Do you feel the same way?"

Syl looked straight at Mom. "I have nothing," she said. "My family is gone. Everything I used to think was important is gone. Matt says he loves me. How can I not love someone who says he loves me?"

I thought about the man Syl had been with. I wondered if he'd said he loved her and if she loved him because he'd said so.

"You will not be dead in six months," Mom said. "None of us will be. Obviously I can't pretend I'm happy about all this. We're long past the point where you'd believe me. But I don't want Matt to leave, and I don't want him to threaten that he's going to every time we get into a fight. We're a family." She paused. "Now the family has one more member," she said. "I would have preferred bridesmaids and rice and a little more warning, but that's just the way it is. We'll have fish for dinner and that box of rice pilaf Miranda found. String beans. A wedding feast."

Matt got up and hugged Mom. "You'll love Syl," he said. "I know you will. Like a daughter."

Given the kinds of fights Mom and I have, I don't think that's a fate Syl will relish.

Chapter 6

May 14

We spent most of the day getting the water out of the cellar. We took turns filling the pails and emptying them. It was a long, disgusting, cruddy day. The electricity never came on, which didn't help.

Two things, though. Syl worked just as hard as the rest of us. And we didn't sing, so I guess we're not crazy.

May 15

Matt and Syl biked to town today to get our food, and to see if they could get more now that Syl's a member of the family, and to ask the mayor to make her an even more official member.

Jon and I volunteered to go with them. "I could be your bridesmaid," I said to Syl, "and make Mom happy."

But what made Mom happy was keeping Jon and me home to do our schoolwork. I guess the somewhat more official wedding day of our brother didn't justify ignoring algebra and Shakespeare.

Mom didn't supervise us, though. She spent the day in Matt's bedroom, cleaning it. Matt's been too impatient to bother.

"We should be going through houses," I said to Jon. "We're going to need more toilet paper now that Syl's here."

"Another bike, too," Jon said. "People left all kinds of good stuff behind."

"I don't suppose they left any steak," I said. "I'm getting tired of shad."

"How do you think I feel?" Jon asked. "It's all we ate last week."

I'd been so taken aback by Syl's existence, I hadn't thought about what she'd be eating. The shad's made a huge difference. Instead of sharing a can of this and a can of that and a can of something else, we've had a can of this and a can of that and some fish. But the shad can't last forever, and then we'll be back to a can of this and a can of that and a can of something else. Only with one more mouth to feed.

All of which was a lot more on my mind than <u>Romeo and Juliet</u> when Matt and Syl got back.

"The mayor wasn't there," Matt said. "Mr. Danworth said he'd tell him to come next Monday, so we'll go back then."

"What about food?" I asked. "Will they give us an extra bag?"

"Not this week," Matt said. "Maybe next week if there's enough. It doesn't matter. Syl and I can share my food."

"No," Mom said. "Syl's a member of this family, so we'll all share."

"That's fine, Mom," Matt said. "But I don't want you eating less so the rest of us can have more."

"Share and share alike," I said, picturing what that would be like once the fish supply runs out. Oh, well. I'm used to being hungry.

"We could go back to the river tomorrow," Jon said. "Matt and Syl and me, and catch some more fish."

"We should," Matt said. "I don't know how much longer the shad will be running, but we should get as much as we can. Syl and I will go. Jon can stay home with you and Miranda."

"I never get to go anyplace," I grumbled.

"Jon, you go with Matt," Mom said. "Syl will stay home with Miranda and me so we can get to know each other better."

"Mom," Matt said, and he sounded exactly like me. I guess whining is a family trait.

"I think that's a good idea," Syl said. "Besides, you'll catch more fish if you aren't distracted."

Jon snickered. Matt looked like he couldn't decide who to kill first.

"We'll leave first thing tomorrow morning," he said. "And get back Wednesday night."

"No," Mom said. "Stay until Friday. Jon's algebra's a lost cause, and the longer you're there, the more fish you'll bring home."

"Mom," Matt said, "could you and I talk about this privately?"

"There's nothing to discuss," Mom said. "You and Jon do the hunter-gatherer thing. Syl and Miranda can roam around the neighborhood looking for boxes of rice pilaf. I'll stay home and worry about all of you. That's the appropriate division of labor."

Syl burst out laughing, but when none of us joined her, she stopped.

"Come on, Matt," Jon said. "We'd better catch lots of fish before we start chopping firewood again."

For a moment I felt sorry for Matt. In an ordinary world he wouldn't have to leave his wife of four days to go fishing with his kid brother. Then again, in an ordinary world he wouldn't have exchanged vows with a strange girl the day after meeting her. At least I assume not.

"Tomorrow morning," Matt said. "And back Friday. After that Syl and I will never be separated again. Is that understood?"

"Nobody's suggesting otherwise," Mom said. This time Syl knew better than to laugh.

So tomorrow Matt and Jon will be leaving again. Who knows. Maybe when they get back, Jon'll have a wife of his own.

May 16

Syl and I went house hunting right after breakfast. I guess she was glad to be away from Mom. I know I was.

"Matt tells me you keep a diary," Syl said as we biked down the road.

"Yeah," I said. "It's only for me, though. No one else reads it."

"I know," Syl said. "It's just funny to think of someone writing about me."

"Didn't you ever keep a diary?" I asked.

"For school once," she said. "But I made up stuff."

"Why?" I asked. "Were things going on you didn't want people to know about?"

"Nothing was going on," Syl said. "Nothing ever went on. But I felt if I put my thoughts down on paper, they wouldn't belong to me anymore."

I'd never thought of it that way, and I didn't think I wanted to. Mom, Matt, and Jon have always respected my privacy, or at least the privacy of my diaries. We don't have any other privacy. It feels strange sharing the sunroom with Jon but not Matt. Less crowded but more intimate somehow.

"I can't get over your hair," I said. "How long it is. How pretty."

"Hair is an asset," Syl said. "You should grow yours."

"Maybe someday," I said. Someday when water isn't gray.

We rode silently for a while, and I waited for Syl to ask me questions the way Jon said she did. But I guess I wasn't as interesting as baseball.

It didn't matter. Once we started breaking into houses, I could see how good Syl was at things. At Mom's insistence we entered each house together, but thanks to Syl, there wasn't a wasted moment. We went through a dozen houses, top to bottom, inch by inch, garages and sheds included. We didn't find that much, and we didn't celebrate when we did find something. No bursting into song over half a roll of toilet paper.

We did find two electric space heaters, though, one for each of us to bike home with. Now, if we ever have electricity, we'll be able to warm up the kitchen and the dining room.

When we got back home, I went up to my room and hid all my diaries in the back of my closet. They're my thoughts and I want to keep them that way.

May 17

I wish Syl hadn't said anything about my diary. I can't blame Matt for telling her, but I really wish he hadn't.

I'm writing this entry in the kitchen using one of the flashlight pens Jon found for me. Mom's asleep in the sunroom, not that it ever mattered before. I've written in my diary with her and Matt and Jon in the room for months now. But even though I know Syl's in Matt's room probably asleep, I feel like somebody's looking over my shoulder.

Last summer Dad and Lisa were here, on their way out west. With six of us in the house I felt more private than I do right now with just three of us here.

Not that I have anything to write, except to say these diaries are mine, for my eyes only.

May 18

Today's the first anniversary of the asteroid hitting the moon.

A year ago I was sixteen years old, a sophomore in high school. Matt was in his freshman year at Cornell and Jon was in middle school. Dad and Lisa had asked me to be godmother to their new baby. Mom was between book projects.

I know I've gained a lot in the past year, but I woke up this morning and all I could think about was everything I've lost. No, that's not right. Not everything, everybody. Everything doesn't matter, not really. After a while you get used to being cold, and hungry, and living in the dark.

But you can't get used to losing people. Or if you can, I don't want to. So many people in the past year, people I've loved, have vanished from my life. Some have died; others have moved on. It almost doesn't matter. Gone is gone.

I was lying on my mattress in the sunroom, thinking about how today was the first anniversary and whether I should mention it to Mom. I know dates because of my diary, but calendars vanished along with everything else during the past year. Somehow I felt the anniversary was like the mound of bodies, the kind of thing you keep to yourself.

But the one thing I've gained this past year is a sister-in-law, and over breakfast this morning (a shared can of sweet potatoes, not the breakfast I had a year ago), Syl brought up the subject.

"Today's the first anniversary," she said.

"Of what?" Mom asked. "Oh, it's been a week since you and Matt exchanged your vows. Well, he'll be back tomorrow and you can celebrate then."

"No, Mom," I said. "Today's the first anniversary of when everything happened. It happened a year ago today."

"Has it only been a year?" Mom asked. "Time sure passes when you're having fun."

"May 18th," Syl said. "I've been keeping track of the days for a while now. I felt I should do something significant on the anniversary day."

"Significant like what?" I asked. "You got married a week ago. It's hard to be more significant than that."

"Something more global," Syl said. "Maybe an offering to the moon goddess."

"Not my firstborn," Mom said. "He's not available."

Syl laughed. "I'm not about to sacrifice Matt," she said. "But there must be something we could give up. Something that matters, that Diana will accept."

"Diana's the goddess of the hunt," Mom said. It always amazes me she knows stuff like that.

"She's also the goddess of the moon," Syl said, proving she had every bit as much useless information as Mom did. "Apollo, god of the sun, is her brother."

"Maybe he's the one we should make an offering to," I

suggested. "We need sunlight a lot more than we need moonlight."

Syl shook her head. "It all began with the moon," she said. "We should start there."

I looked around the sunroom. Horton was sleeping by the woodstove. He's gotten thinner the past couple of weeks, but I wasn't about to offer him to any goddess.

"Maybe Jon's baseball card collection?" I said. "Diana might like a Mickey Mantle rookie card."

"No," Syl said. "The offering has to come from us. We're Diana's handmaidens."

"I know," I said. "We'll give Diana some fish."

"No," Mom said. "We need that fish. Diana can eat out on her own dime."

Syl looked at us. "What do you cherish most?" she asked.

"My children," Mom said. "After them my home. And they're all off limits to Diana, Apollo, and any other god who might happen by."

"My diaries," I said.

"No," Mom said. "Off limits also."

I had mixed feelings about that. Mrs. Nesbitt, I remembered, burned all her letters before she died. Not that I'm planning to die in the immediate future, but if I burned my diaries, I wouldn't have to worry about Syl reading them.

"I don't mind," I said.

"I do," Mom said. "Your diaries are the only record of this family's existence. They're our link to the past and the future. I won't let you destroy them. Not on a whim."

"I don't have anything else," I said, thinking about how pathetic my life was, that I didn't have a single possession worthy of an offering to a goddess I hadn't known existed ten minutes before. "Oh, I do have some trophies, from when I skated. Maybe Diana would like those."

"One trophy," Mom said. "That third-place one you got. The tacky one."

I ran upstairs to my bedroom and found the tacky third-place trophy. I clutched it for a moment, thinking about that competition. I'd fallen twice. If I'd only fallen once, I might have come in second, but the girl who won was really good, and there was no way I could have gotten first.

I'd been ten. Mom and Dad were there, and even Dad, who loved to encourage all of us to do better at our sports, could see the difference in quality between me and the girl who won. On the drive home, instead of talking about my practicing more and harder, he said how proud he was of me, the way I'd gotten up after both falls and continued to skate well enough to medal.

I held on to the trophy and thought about what life had been like when Mom and Dad were still married, when I thought the worst thing that could possibly happen was falling during a competition. I'd been so young, so dumb, upset only that falling twice had cost me the silver.

I went back to the sunroom and found Mom and Syl discussing the appropriate ceremony. "I can't believe you're agreeing to all this," I said to Mom.

"I don't see why not," she said. "I did sillier things in college. I've decided to sacrifice my first book contract. Stay here while I go look for it."

I put the trophy on the floor and sat on my mattress.

"Your mother is amazing," Syl said. "I thought she'd be all righteous about this. No pagan practices, if you know what I mean."

I shrugged. "I don't think Mom believes in much of anything," I said. "And it's not like we really think the moon's going to zip back into place just because we give it a tacky trophy."

"It's a beautiful trophy," Syl said, walking over and picking it up. "You must have been very proud when you won it."

"Not really," I said. "Mom's book contract is a much bigger offering. First book, firstborn, that kind of thing."

"I have to give up something as well," Syl said.

"You didn't come with a lot of stuff," I said.

Syl laughed. "I travel light," she said.

"I'm sure Diana will understand," I said. "Besides, she'll be so dazzled by my trophy, she won't notice anything else."

"She'd better notice my contract," Mom said, joining us. "At least she should appreciate how quickly I found it. You may not believe this, Syl, but I used to be a very organized person."

"I know what I can offer," Syl said, her eyes lighting up. "My hair."

"No!" I cried. "You can't cut your hair. It's an asset."

"I don't need it anymore," Syl said. "Matt loves me, not my hair. Well, not just my hair. Where are your scissors?"

"Do you really think you should?" Mom asked. "Your hair is so beautiful."

"So is Miranda's trophy," Syl said. "So is your contract. They're things that matter. Where do you keep the scissors?"

Mom shook her head, but I got the scissors and brought them to Syl. "I won't be able to cut your braid," I said. "It's too thick."

"Don't worry," Syl said. She unbraided her hair and then took the scissors from me and whacked away. By the time she was finished, her hair looked ragged, the same as Mom's and mine, but her cheekbones looked even better.

Life really is unfair.

"Now what?" Mom said. "We can't make a burnt offering out of Miranda's trophy."

"Let's bury everything," Syl said. "I'm sure Diana will understand."

I wasn't too sure about that. The last thing I want is for the moon to get any closer because of a simple misunderstanding.

"I have a gift bag somewhere," Mom said. "Left over from last Christmas. No, Christmas before last. I keep bows in it. Hold on, I'll get it."

"I'm going to the bathroom to look in the mirror," Syl said. "It's been years since I had short hair."

Horton and I stayed in the sunroom until they got back. Horton didn't seem at all interested in offerings, so I didn't ask him if he'd be willing to give up his favorite catnip mouse.

Mom and Syl came back, and we put the trophy in the bag first, and then the contract around it, and stuffed in Syl's hair.

"There should be a shovel in the garage," Mom said. "Miranda, get it, and you girls can bury everything by the window. I'll stay inside where it's warm."

"Join us—" Syl said, and she stopped in such a funny way, Mom and I both understood the problem immediately.

"Call me Laura," Mom said. "And thank you, but I'd just as soon watch from here."

I went to the garage and got the shovel, and then Syl came out with the bag. We picked a spot where it would be easy for Mom to see us, and we took turns shoveling. All the snow is melted now and the ground is soft, so it didn't take much effort. Besides, I folded the bag over, so it wasn't very big.

I thought about how hard it had been for me to pray by the mound of bodies, and I realized if I couldn't pray there, I didn't want to pray to a goddess. "You say something," I said to Syl. "I'll pray silently."

"All right," Syl said. "Oh, Diana, goddess of the moon. Take our offerings and return peace and wholeness to our planet."

I thought about the earth then, really thought about it, the tsunamis and earthquakes and volcanoes, all the horrors I haven't witnessed but have changed my life, the lives of everyone I know, all the people I'll never know. I thought about life without the sun, the moon, stars, without flowers and warm days in May. I thought about a year ago and all the good things I'd taken for granted and all the unbearable things that had replaced those simple blessings. And even though I hated the thought of crying in front of Syl, tears streamed down my face.

"That's good," she said, gently wiping my cheeks. "Your tears are the best offering of all."

May 19

It was an awful day.

It started raining last night and it never stopped. It was cold and windy, and the combination made me realize we haven't had electricity in a week or more. All those lovely electric heaters are useless.

We had no idea when Matt and Jon would get back, but we knew they'd have a hard trip because of the rain. Mom checked on the cellar to see if it was flooded, and she cursed so loudly, Syl and I could hear her from the sunroom.

Horton's hardly eaten since Jon left, but in spite of that he managed to throw up a hairball. Even though we've been cooking the shad on the barbecue outside, the sunroom stinks of fish. Two aspirin did nothing for my headache.

Matt and Jon got in around 4:00. Last week they brought back two huge bags of fish and a sister-in-law. This time all they had was a half bag.

"We stayed as long as we could," Jon said. "There was hardly any fish. Everyone was gone."

"Put on some dry clothes," Mom said. "We'll be fine with what you caught."

But we all knew we wouldn't be. We'll go through the fish in no time, and then it'll be five people with food for four. I can tell myself over and over that I'm used to being hungry, that it isn't so bad, but it is bad and I hate it. I just hate being cold and lonely and dirty more.

The first thing Matt did was go to Syl and hug her so hard I thought she'd choke. "I kept thinking what if you're not here," he said. "What if you left while I was gone?"

"Why would I do that?" Syl asked, which wasn't exactly the same as "I love you and need you and will never ever leave you."

Matt pulled away from her and then he noticed. "What did you do to your hair?" he said. "Mom, did you make Syl cut her hair off? Was it so she should look like shit, the same as the rest of us?"

"No, Matt," I said. "Mom tried to talk her out of it." It didn't seem like the right time to explain about offerings to the moon goddess Diana.

"I was tired of it," Syl said. "It was a nuisance to keep clean. Besides, this way I look like I belong."

"You don't belong," Matt said. "Don't you understand? I love you because you're different from everything I've been stuck with this past year."

"I'm sick of you, too!" Jon shouted. "I don't want to be in this stupid family, either!"

"Matt, you go upstairs," Mom said. "You and Syl both. Take your fight to your room. And change into dry clothes while you're up there."

"Mom, you can't keep telling me what we should do," Matt said.

"Yes, I can," Mom said. "As long as you live under my roof. Now go!"

Syl took Matt's hand and led him out.

"Miranda, take the bag of fish and put it in the garage," Mom said. "Now."

"Can I put my coat on first?" I asked.

"No back talk!" Mom said. "Get out."

I grabbed the pathetic half-full bag of smelly, disgusting, uncleaned fish and went out into the cold, dreary, rainy day. When I got to the garage (which in all honesty took about ten seconds), I realized I didn't have the key to the padlock. I was stuck outside in the cold, dreary rain until Mom came to her senses.

I didn't know how long it would take Matt to fall in love with shorthaired Syl, but my guess was once he noticed her cheekbones, he'd adjust. Which meant the two of them would resume their honeymoon and it'd be a while before we saw them again. Which was fine with me.

But what I really couldn't be sure of was how long Mom would need to talk with Jon. And even though my head hurt, and I hate shad, and I was cold and wet and hungry and scared, I knew Jon was cold and wet and hungry and scared and really angry at Matt, who must have made his life miserable for the past few days.

So I stood against the garage wall with the bag of shad by my side. It began raining really hard then. There was no way to keep dry, and I began to shiver.

"It'd serve them right if I died of pneumonia," I said to myself, because when you're stuck outside in the rain with half a bag of dead fish, you say stupid things like that out loud.

I thought about pulling the shad out of the bag and counting them, multiplying by two, for the two remaining bags, then dividing the total by five, so I could guess how short a time it would be before all we'd have were a few cans of vegetables to keep us alive.

I thought about the mound of bodies.

I thought about what a really rotten moon goddess Diana had turned out to be.

I wasn't outside for more than ten minutes, but it was long enough that I was shaking pretty badly by the time Jon came to get me. He was carrying my coat and an umbrella.

"Mom says she's sorry," he said.

I knew she was. I knew Matt was, too. I knew we were all sorry. That's what we're best at. Being sorry.

May 20

Last night Jon took the plywood off the dining room window and moved his mattress in. He now has the room to himself, although of course we can look in from the sunroom.

Mom asked me this morning if I wanted to take the plywood off the kitchen window as well. She said she'd keep sleeping in the sunroom and could check on the woodstove during the night.

I considered it, but right now what I really want is to be back in my bedroom. Being there the other day, looking at my skating trophies, made me long for my bed, my chest of drawers, my windows.

The dining room has two doors: one from the living room and one from the kitchen. But we're never in the living room, since that's where we put all the dining room furniture. And there's no reason to go from the kitchen to the dining room, except for Jon to get in there.

But you have to cross the kitchen to get to the downstairs bathroom and the sunroom, and even the cellar stairs. And it's the kitchen. We keep our food there and plates and silverware.

The dining room may only have fake privacy. But the kitchen has no privacy whatsoever.

So I'm going to keep sharing the sunroom with Mom, at least for the time being. We moved our mattresses away from the back door, and then we moved the clothesline into the kitchen so the sunroom feels less like a dorm and more like a family room.

It's rained on and off since Matt and Jon got home. It's not like I expect to see sunlight, but I'd like it if things dried out.

May 21

Just what we needed. A cold spell. The rain turned into snow last night, and there are a couple of fresh inches on the ground.

"Sometimes it snows in the spring," Mom said. "It'll melt soon enough."

Matt and Syl took advantage of the snow day by spending it in Matt's room. Occasionally there were shrieks.

Jon reorganized his baseball cards. Good thing we hadn't sacrificed Mickey Mantle.

I looked out onto the backyard and pictured the mound of bodies covered once again with snow.

Chapter 7

May 22

Matt and Syl came back from town, and Matt was in a much better mood. It couldn't have been easy biking through the snow, but he didn't care.

"The mayor was in, and he performed the ceremony," Matt said, waving a marriage certificate. "Syl and I are now married in the eyes of the great state of Pennsylvania."

"You should have come with us," Syl said. "All of you."

"Maybe next time," Mom said.

"And look," Matt said. "Five bags of food!"

I did look. I looked even harder as Mom and I put the food away. There were a few cans more than last week, but I think what Mr. Danworth did was give us our standard amount and put it in five bags instead of four.

Mom decided, since the fish has been cleaned and salted and is already stinking up the garage, that we should only have it a couple of days a week and then just two shad for the five of us. I'm glad, even though I know she's doing it because she's scared of what's going to happen when we run out and when we no longer get any cans from town.

What will become of us then? Where will we go? Will Matt and Syl leave by themselves and I'll never see him again?

I know I should be happy for him, but with everything I'm scared of, I think I'm scared most of losing Matt forever.

May 23

"Did Horton eat last week?" Jon asked me. "When I was away?"

"A little," I said.

"He isn't eating very much," Jon said.

"Cats eat less in the spring," I said. "Horton always loses his winter weight."

"Yeah, but he's really getting thin," Jon said.

I know he's right, but there's nothing we can do about it. When Horton feels like eating, he'll eat.

May 24

We spent the day drying the cellar out, pail by pail. The electricity came back on for the first time in weeks, and Matt got the sump pump running.

Mom acted like this was Christmas and New Year's. I'm surprised she didn't burst out singing.

May 25

Matt and Jon are back chopping firewood. As far as I'm concerned, that means the official end of the school year.

Nothing good happened to Romeo or Juliet.

May 26

The third day in a row with electricity. All three days the electricity's been on for hours, and last night it came back on for a few hours as well.

We don't get any TV reception, and the news on the radio remains bad, but Mom announced that we should spring clean. So that's how she and Syl and I spent the day. The menfolk chopped wood. Us women vacuumed and scrubbed.

Matt came home exhausted, but when he saw how clean things were, his mood brightened. "Syl, you're fantastic," he said.

Syl worked every bit as hard as Mom and me but no harder.

Sometimes I'd like to kill him.

May 27

I can't remember the last time I was in a good mood. It feels like all I do is crab and mope and feel sorry for myself.

Since the house is as close to spotless as it's ever going to get and Romeo and Juliet are totally dead, I told Mom I was going house hunting. I think she was glad to get me out of here, so she didn't put up a battle.

"I'll go, too," Syl said, which wasn't my idea at all. "Laura, do you want to come with us?"

Thank goodness Mom said no. "See if you can find any more books for me," she said instead.

I didn't want to go house hunting with Syl. I wanted to spend time by myself. I was looking for a tactful way of explaining that to Syl, but before I could, she said, "Let's split up. We can meet here at noon."

"How will you find your way back?" I asked. Matt would kill me if I let Syl out of my sight and she wandered off, never to be seen again.

"I never get lost," Syl said. "I'll be back here. Don't worry."

I thought about how lost I'd gotten and I've lived here practically my whole life. But Syl's an old married woman and I'm just the kid sister-in-law. And I really did want some alone time. "Fine," I said. "I'll see you, then."

We biked together until Schiller Road, and she turned to the left. I kept biking down Howell Bridge Road until the right onto Penn Avenue. Lots of nice houses there. A very literate neighborhood.

I really do love breaking and entering, and I got positively cheery seeing how the wealthier people in Howell used to live. Not that I found that much we could use, since everybody else must have realized Penn Ave. would have good pickings.

But there were books for Mom, and one space heater, and best of all, two pairs of blue jeans, price tags still attached, in a size I never could have fit in before. I tried on one pair, and it was a little loose (I guess shad doesn't have that many calories) but definitely wearable. Syl weighs even less than I do, but I figured the second pair could stay up with a belt, and I was sure she'd appreciate having something new to wear.

I also took a can of ocean breeze room freshener. Now that the temperature's up to 50, Mom's been opening the windows to air the house out, but everything smells like fish anyway. That and a travel-sized bottle of aspirin were my best finds.

I balanced the handlebars with one trash bag on one side and one on the other and began biking to the rendezvous spot. My mood was much better than it has been in ages. I pictured how pleased Syl would be with my gift of blue jeans, and how Matt would appreciate my generosity, and how Mom would love the books I'd found, and how Jon . . . Well, how Jon would turn out to be a secret ocean breeze air freshener freak. Okay, I couldn't think of why anything I brought home would make Jon happy, except maybe the aspirin, for when his muscles ache from chopping wood.

Jon's never been easy to shop for.

Even with nobody to hear me for miles, I didn't burst into song, but I did whistle as I biked. I liked the splashy way the bike rode through puddles on the road. And I had this great realization: I don't have to be happy all the time. With everything that's happened, no one should expect to be happy. But moments of happiness can sneak up on you, like pairs of unworn blue jeans, and you need to cherish them because they're so rare and so unpredictable.

I even understood why Matt married Syl ten minutes after meeting her. Finding her was rare and unpredictable.

Of course it hadn't hurt that she had long hair at the time.

I was whistling "I Dream of Jeannie with the Light Brown Hair," a song I learned in third grade and haven't heard since, when I rode my bike straight into a pothole and went flying off.

I landed face down in a puddle, and for an instant I was in a state of total panic. I remembered Mom in the cellar, and I swear I thought I was going to drown.

What shocked me to my senses was how much I hurt. When you're in that kind of pain, you almost wish you were going to drown in a half inch of water.

I rolled out of the puddle and moved my fingers, my hands, my arms, my legs, until I was satisfied I hadn't broken any bones. The palms of my hands were scraped and it felt like my knees were, too. My chin and jaw hurt horribly, but I wasn't spitting any teeth out. I was going to be a total-body black-and-blue mark, but no one dies of bruises.

I crawled back to the bike. It was lying on its side, but the two trash bags were unbroken, and both tires looked okay.

That was when I realized how lucky I'd been the day I got lost. What if I'd had a flat tire? I'd been miles away from home, with no idea where I was, and I would have had to walk back.

Sometimes I think all I've done for the past month is cry, but that didn't stop me. I sat by my bike, telling myself over and over again how lucky I was, and I sobbed.

I didn't have to use my sweatshirt to blow my nose this time, though. I'd found a tissue packet at one of the houses, so when I was up to it, I dug through a trash bag and located it.

That's progress.

I was just finishing the tissue packet when Syl rode over. We were south of our meeting spot, but she must have looked around for me, and since I was on Howell Bridge Road when I fell, I couldn't have been too hard to locate.

"You're a mess," she said, helping me up.

"I rode into a pothole," I said.

Syl nodded and straightened up my bike. "Which will be easier?" she asked. "Riding or walking?"

Either way, it was going to be a mile uphill. "How about letting me die here?" I asked.

"Laura would never forgive me," Syl said. "Do you need a few more minutes?"

What I needed was a completely different life. "I'll try walking," I said. "I'm feeling too wobbly for the bike."

"All right," Syl said. She grabbed the handlebars of her bike with her right hand and the handlebars of mine with her left, and began pulling them behind her, while I hobbled by her side.

"You'll be all right," she said after a few of the most agonizing yards I've ever walked. "You couldn't make it this far if anything was broken."

Just because I knew it was true didn't make me any happier to hear it.

"I remember once, months ago," Syl said. "Right after the air got bad. The band I was with—"

"You were with a band?" I asked.

"Not that kind of band," Syl said. "When you're on the road, you find bands of people to travel with. By foot, by bike, even by truck."

"There are trucks?" I said. I couldn't remember the last time I saw a truck.

"Of course there are," Syl said. "How do you think food gets to Howell? And they're always bringing supplies to the safe towns. They're not supposed to give people lifts, but sometimes they do."

"Were you with a band of people when you met Matt?" I asked.

"Just one other person," Syl said. "We'd split off because he wanted to try fishing in the Delaware. Anyway, this happened last summer. We were in South Carolina, I think. There were a half dozen of us, and we saw a man lying on the side of the road. You could tell right away his leg was broken, and he was screaming in pain."

"Did you do anything?" I asked.

"There was nothing we could do," Syl said. "Even if we'd set his leg, we couldn't carry him with us. If you can't keep up with a band, you get left behind. People died all the time, but mostly when they were dying, they were quiet or moaning. This guy must have broken his leg right before we saw him. He was going to lie there on the side of the road for days before he died. He knew it. We all knew it. Eventually he'd pass out, but until then he was going to scream because he was in agony and because he knew he was going to die."

"And you left him there?" I asked.

"One of the guys I was with said we should put him down," Syl said. "Maybe someone else did. We didn't stick around to find out."

"Did you ever tell Matt that story?" I asked.

"No," Syl said. "I haven't thought about it in months. It was the way your bike was overturned that made me think of it. One of the guys I was with took the bike and rode off. If you had a bike, you didn't stay with people who were walking."

"Would I have gotten left behind?" I asked. "I mean, after a fall like I took just now. If I couldn't keep up with everyone else?"

"Oh yeah," Syl said. "Sure. But you would have found another group in a day or so. There were always groups of people to grab on to."

I hated the story of the guy with the broken leg, but I kind of liked the image of all these groups wandering around together. When you've shared a room with the same three people for months, fresh faces sound appealing.

We walked in silence for a while, and I fantasized about a group of good-looking guys and me. It's a good thing I have a permanently gray complexion or else Syl might have noticed how hard I was blushing.

Mom wasn't too happy when she saw how I looked, but she found some peroxide and cleaned my palms and knees. Suddenly, I was six years old again and had fallen off my bike.

She was glad for the books, though, and Syl appreciated the blue jeans. Jon didn't say anything about the air freshener, so maybe ocean breeze isn't his favorite.

May 28

The worst night I can remember in ages.

I've been having nightmares for a couple of weeks now, ever since I got lost. Horrible dreams about the mound of bodies. A lot of times I see us in the mound, or I think I'm with Mom and then I look around and there's the mound and I have to climb on top of it to find her.

Twice I had dreams that I was in Mrs. Nesbitt's house after she died, and I'm looking around for things and wherever I turn, there she is. Both times I woke up thinking Mrs. Nesbitt was still alive, and I had to remind myself that she was dead and I had gone through her house, with her body lying on her bed, and that I had believed at the time it was okay to do that.

One dream I had was so much like a horror movie, it was almost funny. Mrs. Nesbitt and I were playing tennis (which is a funny thought right there), and I looked up at the stands and everyone watching the match was dead. Nobody I knew, though. They all looked like ghouls.

I don't know if I've been in a bad mood because of the nightmares or if I'm having the nightmares because I'm in a bad mood. Probably both. I know I haven't been sleeping well, and that hasn't helped.

But last night I had nightmare after nightmare. I don't know if I ever woke up. It felt like one dream led directly to another. In one I was going through someone's house and I opened a closet door and piles of corpses fell out. Then I was in the same house and I opened a different door and the dead people were all people I knew. Then I saw Mom sitting in a rocking chair, and she said, "Don't look at me like I'm dead," only she <u>was</u> dead.

But then I had the worst dream—maybe the worst dream I've had in my life. I was walking to school and everything was normal, the way it had been. The sun was shining, and I remember how happy I felt seeing the sun again. I wasn't sure if everything was back to normal or if none of the bad things had ever happened. It didn't matter. The sun was shining, and I was walking to school. The closer I got to town, the more people I saw. Everybody was happy, so I realized the sun had returned. We were all celebrating because we could see the sun again.

Then I heard someone screaming, and I looked down at a man, his leg twisted horribly. I knew right away it was the man with the broken leg Syl had told me about. It was like I wasn't asleep anymore because I thought, Oh, that's the guy Syl mentioned. Then I thought the man was Dad, which was when the dream turned into a nightmare. But I realized it wasn't anyone I knew, and I remember thinking, Okay, this isn't going to be another nightmare after all.

I felt like I was awake and this was all truly happening.

Everyone who was walking stopped, and some of the people came back. There must have been ten or fifteen of us standing around the guy, who kept screaming. Someone said, "Shut up already," and kicked the man in his leg.

Then other people started kicking him, and—this is the worst part—I started kicking him, too. I thought, If I don't join in, they'll kick me. But part of me enjoyed it, because I was okay and this guy, who somehow represented everything that had been awful for the past year, was lying there helpless.

The more we kicked, the louder he screamed, and the more excited I got.

In my sleep I thought, This dream is going to turn and I'm going to be the person lying on the ground, but that never happened. I guess I woke up before it could. I know I was shaking when I woke up. My body hurts all over from the fall, but I swear my leg hurt even more, like it ached from kicking.

A month ago I was dreaming about Baby Rachel. Dreams I thought were scary.

For the first time ever I hoped there was no Baby Rachel. I don't know what happened to Dad and Lisa, if the baby was ever born. It must be so hard now to have a baby. Lisa could have miscarried or had a stillborn baby. Horrible though that is, it might be for the better.

I tiptoed out of the sunroom and through the kitchen to the bathroom. It smells of fish and bedpans and ocean breeze air freshener. I curled up on the cold tile floor, and I rocked back and forth, glad it made my body ache even more, like I deserved the punishment for what I'd been thinking.

I hate my dreams. I hate Matt for bringing Syl into our lives, and I hate Syl for giving me her nightmares.

I hate this world we live in.

June

June 1

The doorbell rang.

Mom and I sat there, frozen by the sound. Syl was upstairs napping. Matt and Jon were chopping firewood.

The doorbell rang again.

Mom gestured for me to stay absolutely still.

"Laura? Laura? Are you in there? It's me, Lisa!"

"Oh my God," Mom said. "Lisa?" She raced to the back door and opened it. "Lisa? Is that really you?"

Lisa was crying. "Please," she said. "Please let me in."

"Of course," Mom said, and gathered Dad's wife in her arms. "Oh, Lisa. I'm sorry. I'm in a state of shock."

"Where's Dad?" I asked. "Is he here? Is he all right?"

"Yes, yes, he's out front with the baby," Lisa said. "Everyone's outside. Hal thought it would be safer if I came first, that it wouldn't frighten you as much if you heard a woman's voice."

At least I think that's what she said, because before she was halfway through, I had run through the house, passing Syl on the stairway, and flung the front door open. There he was: my father, still alive, home where I could hold him and never let him go.

"Miranda, Miranda," he said. "I knew this day would come. I never lost hope."

"Oh, Daddy," I said, and the tears streaming down my face were tears of joy for a change. "I don't believe it. I can't. It's too good to be true."

Dad laughed. "It's true all right," he said. He turned to one of the other people he was with, a girl, I noticed, and took a baby from her arms. "Meet Gabriel," he said, handing the baby to me.

I was so stunned the baby's name wasn't Rachel, I almost didn't reach out. Gabrielle's a pretty name, I told myself. It was <u>my</u> fantasy she'd be named Rachel, no one else's.

Dad was beaming. "This is Miranda, your sister and your godmother," he said to the baby. "Miranda, this is your baby brother Gabriel."

I looked down at the baby I was cradling. "It's a boy?" I said.

"He was born right after midnight on Christmas Day," Dad said.

For months now I've dreamed of my little sister, Baby Rachel. A few days ago I was in such despair, I'd hoped she'd never been born. And now I was holding that very baby, only it was a boy and it was screaming.

"He cries a lot," the girl said. "You get used to it."

Lisa and Mom had come to the front door. "Come in, everyone," Mom said. "Syl's gone to get the boys. Please, come in. You can warm up in the sunroom while I make a pot of tea."

Lisa took the baby, Gabriel, from my arms, and for the first time I really looked at the people Dad was with. They were unloading their backpacks and taking their coats off, so they didn't seem to notice that I was staring at them.

There were five altogether, if you count Dad and Lisa. Six if you include the baby. Besides Dad, there were two guys: one maybe in his thirties, the other one more my age or Matt's. The girl who'd been holding the baby looked young, close to Jon's age. Everyone's so thin nowadays, and gray and sad, you can't really tell ages anymore. Except the older guy wasn't thin. He wasn't exactly robust, but he certainly wasn't thin.

We followed Mom into the sunroom. "It's so warm in here," the younger guy said.

We had the woodstove going, of course, and one of the electric heaters was on. Mom has it in her head we'll use less firewood that way.

"Please," Mom said. "Make yourselves comfortable. Lisa, is there anything I can do for the baby?"

"He's hungry," she said, and she began to nurse him. The other people—their band, I guessed—acted like this was the most normal thing in the world.

I didn't have to figure out where to look, since Syl, Matt, and Jon burst in. Jon held on to Dad even longer than I had, and then Matt got his turn to hug Dad.

"This is Syl," Matt told them. "My wife."

"Your wife?" Dad said, giving Matt an extra congratulatory hug. "When did that happen?"

"Three weeks ago," Matt said.

"May I kiss the bride?" Dad asked, but he didn't wait for an answer. Instead he gave Syl a hug, which she resisted for a second, but then responded to with a hug and a peck on Dad's cheek.

"Can you believe it?" Dad asked. "My son got married."

"Congratulations," the older of the two men said, and gave Matt his hand to shake. "That's wonderful news. Hal talks so much about you, but he never once guessed he had a daughter-in-law."

"Are you from around here, Syl?" Dad asked. "Did Matt go to school with you?"

"No," Syl said. "We met nearby."

"That's great," Dad said. "Lisa, darling, can you believe it? Matt's married."

"And you had your baby," Matt said.

"A boy," I said. "Gabriel."

"I have a baby brother?" Jon said. "Wow."

Dad laughed. "It's all wow," he said. "Oh, I'm sorry. There are introductions to make. It's just—well, I know you understand. Laura, everyone, this is Charlie Rutherford, and Alex and Julie Morales. And in case you haven't figured it out, this is Laura, the mother of my beautiful children Matt, Miranda, and Jon. And now Syl, my unexpected daughter-in-law."

There we were, eleven of us, crowded into the sunroom. If Alex Morales had thought it was warm before, our body heat and the lingering smell of fish now made it almost unbearable.

"It takes a while for the kettle to boil," Mom said. "Please, everybody, sit down. Miranda, get the mugs, and the tea bags."

I went into the kitchen. The girl, Julie, followed me. "Let me help," she said. I gave her a couple of mugs to carry in.

Mom's been using her tea bags over and over again, but she's down to her last half dozen. Now five of them would be used.

Did Dad expect us to feed all these people? Sure, he and Lisa were entitled to whatever we could give them, but the others were strangers to us. And on a Thursday. If we fed them the way we usually ate, we'd be out of food by Saturday.

I thought I saw Alex give a quick look at Julie. "Just hot water for Julie and me, please," he said, handing one of the mugs to Dad.

"It's just boiled rainwater," Mom said.

"But it's in a cup," Julie said. "And in a warm room."

Charlie laughed. He had a big man's laugh, and it changed the atmosphere immediately. "See how little it takes to make us happy?" he said. "This is very kind of you, Mrs. Evans."

"Laura, please," Mom said. "I only wish I could offer you more. Miranda, get the bottle of lemon extract. That will give the water a bit of flavor."

I ran back into the kitchen, found the extract, and returned it to the sunroom. I bumped into Alex as I did, and I blushed while I apologized.

"My fault," he said. "I was in your way."

I glanced at him, trying to act like I wasn't looking. He reminded me a little of Syl, like he'd always been thin, like his body was used to it. His eyes were a very dark brown. I used to like more athletic boys, but I could see that he'd be good-looking under ordinary circumstances.

But these aren't ordinary circumstances, and even though I couldn't get over the idea that a guy had fallen into my sunroom, I was a lot more excited about Dad coming home.

"How's Grandma?" I asked. "Did you get to her?"

"And what about your parents, Lisa?" Mom asked. "Are they all right?"

Lisa had finished feeding the baby and was patting him gently.

"Let me," Charlie said, and Lisa gave Gabriel to him.

"We never got out west," Dad said. "We don't know."

"It was horrible," Lisa said. "We went from one evac camp to another, for as long as I could manage. Then the flu hit. By the time they lifted the quarantine, I was too far along to travel."

"Everyone tried," Dad said. "Lisa got extra food because she was pregnant. There were some great people: doctors, nurses, sacrificing their lives to help others. But by the time Gabriel was born, we'd been told not to try to go farther west. They said there was no point: Colorado, Nevada, were devastated. What survivors there were had been moved east or south."

"We thought about you all the time," I said. "Hoping and worrying."

"You were never out of our thoughts," Dad said. "Our thoughts and our prayers."

"Was Gabriel really born on Christmas?" I asked.

"He sure was," Charlie said. "I was there." Gabriel was holding on to his ring finger with a possessive grip.

"Are you a doctor?" Matt asked.

Charlie laughed again. "Not hardly," he said. "I was a telemarketer back in the day."

We all laughed at the very thought of telemarketers.

"We met at the evac camp," Dad said. "Charlie was great, helping everybody, boosting morale."

"You make it sound like a prison camp," Matt said. He was clutching Syl's hand. I wonder what she's told him about her time on the road.

"In some ways it was like a prison camp," Dad said. "Especially during the quarantine. There was never enough food, or blankets, or medicine. But we held on, and Lisa had the baby, and thank God, they both came through."

"Did you all meet there?" Jon asked. "I'm sorry. I've forgotten your names."

"Alex and Julie Morales," Alex said. "No. We met later, maybe two months ago? Time loses a lot of its meaning."

"Lisa and I had decided to come back," Dad said. "She knew how important it was for me to be with my children, all my children. Charlie came along because by then we couldn't imagine life without him. He's the best friend we've ever had. We ran into Alex and Julie, who were making their way back east, also."

"You've stuck together all this time?" Syl asked.

"I know," Dad said. "It's unusual. In some ways we've become a family. Other people came and went, but the five of us held on."

"Hal and Lisa have been kind to us," Alex said. "Very protective of Julie."

"She's worth protecting," Charlie said. "You both are."

"I know it's an imposition, Laura," Dad said. "Us barging in on you like this. To be perfectly honest, I haven't thought what our next step should be."

"Julie and I won't be staying," Alex said. "We have other plans."

Dad held his hand up to stop him. "Julie's exhausted," he said. "Look at her. She's already fallen asleep. You need time to recover before you move on."

I held my breath, waiting for Mom's response to all this. It was one thing for me to be thrilled that Dad was back. It was another for her to welcome her ex-husband, his wife and baby, and three strangers.

"You caught us at a good time," Mom said. "Matt and Jon have spent the past few weeks fishing in the Delaware."

"No kidding," Dad said. "The shad were running?"

"We got our share," Matt said.

"Enough for all of us, at least for a few days," Mom said. "We have some cans of food, too. There've been government handouts. We get food on Monday."

"Maybe they'll let Dad have some," Jon said. "Like they gave some to Syl."

"Well, we won't know that until Monday," Mom said. "But if you don't mind eating fish for the next few days, I don't see why you can't stay here."

"Oh, Laura," Dad said.

"You and Lisa and the baby can sleep in the sunroom," Mom said. "We can't count on electricity, but the wood-stove will keep you warm. That will be best for the baby. Julie can share the kitchen with Miranda and me, and Jon, Alex, and Charlie can sleep in the dining room. Between the mattresses and the sleeping bags and the blankets, we should manage all right."

"This is very kind of you, Laura," Charlie said. "And you'll see. We're great workers."

"Good," Mom said. "That's settled. Jon, take a plastic bag and go to the garage and bring back some fish. A lot of fish. We'll have to eat in shifts, I'm afraid, but at least we'll all have supper."

"We only eat two meals a day," Matt said.

"Are you kidding?" Alex said. "Two meals a day? That's luxury."

"It is for us, too," Matt said.

"It'll be fine," Mom said. "It'll work out. We'll make it work out."

Last night, I wrote my diary entry in my bedroom closet, the most private place I could think of. Thanks to a couple of the flashlight pens Jon gave me, I had enough light, and although I could hear Matt and Syl murmuring in their room, the only other sound was Gabriel crying.

Gabriel cries a lot.

I hid my diary along with my other diaries, but I got it in my head my hiding place would be too easy to find if anyone really looked. It was hard enough after Matt brought Syl, but Charlie and Alex and Julie are strangers, and who knows what they were like before things happened, or even what they're like now.

So I was in my closet, searching for a better hiding place, which was why I got to hear Mom and Matt arguing in Matt's bedroom.

"They can't stay," Matt said. "You know that."

"This is what I know," Mom said. "I've already told Jon this, and I'll tell Miranda when we have a moment alone. There is only one person in this house who matters and that's the baby. He can't survive without his mother, so that makes Lisa the second most important person. All the rest of us, even the girls, can get by if we have to. Syl's shown me that. But the baby can't, so we have to see to it that Lisa is taken care of, that she has enough to eat, that the baby is kept warm and dry. If that means all those people move into this house, then so be it. If that means we all eat a little less so Lisa can eat a little more, then so be it. No baby is going to die because I ate a second can of green beans. Do you understand me?"

"I do," Matt said. "And on the face of it what you're saying makes sense. But if you're so concerned about that second can of green beans, how can you justify Dad eating it? Let alone all those other people. Mom, Jon and I worked hard for those fish. It wasn't fun and games, especially not the second trip. You know as well as I do the food we're getting from town isn't enough to sustain us, and it sure isn't going to last forever. We need to be as strong as possible when we have to leave here. Just having Dad and Lisa and that army they brought with them here cuts down on our chances. What if the rains stop? Will we fight with them for water?"

"I'm not turning them out," Mom said. "This isn't a way station for Hal. You're his children. He has rights."

"He has no rights!" Matt exploded. "He deserted us twice. He left you years ago—"

"That was a mutual decision," Mom said.

"He left you," Matt said. "You would have kept the marriage going if he hadn't and you know that. And then he and Lisa drop by last summer and go their merry way. We owe them nothing."

"They brought us food," Mom said. "Food that kept us alive for weeks, maybe months. Food they could have kept for themselves. And would things have been better if they'd stayed? Lisa hysterical with worry over her parents? Food running out and then the sickness. Maybe she wouldn't have survived. Maybe the baby would have died. Things could have been so much worse, Matt. I'm not sure they'd have been any better."

"I don't know, Mom," Matt said, and his voice got so much lower I had to strain to hear him. "Maybe you should have let Miranda go with them. That might have been the best thing after all."

I felt like I'd been punched in my stomach. I had never known Dad wanted me along with him and Lisa when they left here last summer.

"Is that what you wish for her?" Mom asked. "Evac camps? A life like Syl's?"

"Leave Syl out of this," Matt said. "She didn't have parents to look after her. Dad would have protected Miranda. Yeah, it would have been hard, but it's been hard for her here. And we knew, we all knew, that whatever food we had would last that much longer with one less mouth to feed."

"I couldn't let her go," Mom said. "I couldn't send Miranda or Jon or you out there knowing I might never see you again. I don't know how those kids' parents could have done it, Alex and Julie's."

"My guess is they don't have parents," Matt said. "Any more than Syl does."

Mom sighed. "This is a horrible time," she said. "But we've gotten through it together, and that's how it's going to be. I'm sure Hal's already thinking about what to do next. In the meantime we'll make do. Lisa isn't going to go hungry while she's nursing. We can't let that happen."

I heard Syl walking up the stairs. "Laura?" she said. "I remembered seeing a flannel sheet in the linen closet. I thought we could cut it up for diapers."

"Good idea," Mom said.

"Stay here for a moment," Matt said. "Mom and I have been talking, and I want you to know what's going on."

I used that chance to slip out of my bedroom and make my way downstairs before anyone realized I might have eavesdropped. My timing was perfect, since as I walked past the living room, I heard an argument between Dad and Lisa.

"We can't let Julie go," Lisa said. "Who knows where Alex will take her, what will become of her."

"We know exactly where she's going," Dad said. "Alex's been very clear about their plans."

"To leave her in an orphanage," Lisa said. "So he can go off to Ohio."

"It's not an orphanage," Dad said. "It's a convent, and it took in girls like Julie last summer. It's not like he's planning to join the circus. He feels that Julie would be safer at the convent than she is on the road."

"But she'd be safe with us!" Lisa cried. "Hal, I don't think I can survive without Julie. She understands what I've gone through. No one else does."

"I do," Dad said. "I wish you'd believe me, Lisa."

"You don't," Lisa said. "You say you do. You may even believe it, but you don't. You decided right away that your mother had died. Even when we were trying to make it out west, you never thought you'd see your mother again. But my whole family was out there—my parents, my sisters. I'll never know if they're alive or dead. All I have is my faith that God will reunite us. Julie knows how that feels, that need to see your family again, that terror that you never will. She's the only one I can talk to."

"You can talk to me," Dad said. "You _are_ talking to me."

"It makes no sense for Julie to live with nuns she's never even met," Lisa said. "If Alex would let her stay with us, then he could do whatever he wants, and he'd never have to worry about her. Please, Hal. Talk to him again, try to convince him. I'm sure the nuns are wonderful women, devout women, but Julie doesn't know them. She knows us. I've lost so much, Hal. God brought Julie to me, to help me through. He can't want me to lose her."

"Are you enjoying yourself?"

I turned around and saw Alex standing there. Who knows how long he'd been watching me.

"I'm not enjoying any of this," I said to him. "Thank you for asking."

"Miranda, is that you?" Dad called.

"Yeah, Dad," I said, sticking my head into the living room, nice and casual. "I was looking for Lisa. I wanted to tell her Syl found a flannel sheet Gabriel can use for diapers. Oh, hi, Lisa. I bet Gabriel will like that, a new set of diapers."

"I know I will," Dad said. "We've been down to four diapers for weeks now. Every night we wash three and hope they'll be dry by the morning."

I imagined quickly what my life would have been like if I'd left with Dad and Lisa back in August. Only I couldn't imagine. Maybe if I'd gone, Mom, Matt, and Jon would have left before winter got bad. Maybe I never would have seen them again, and I'd be like Lisa, not knowing if my family was still alive, only without her faith. Or maybe I'd have her faith. Lisa hadn't been particularly religious that I could remember.

"I saw some textbooks, Miranda," Alex said. "Julie's in eighth grade. Would it be all right if we used some of your books?"

"They're ninth grade textbooks," I said, like that would make a difference. "Sure. Jon's stopped using them, at least for the summer."

"We have a Bible," Lisa said. "Julie can read from that."

Alex smiled at her. "Yes, she can," he said. "Julie and I read from our missal. But it would be good for her to review spelling and grammar and math. She was a very good student when she went to Holy Angels."

I was starting to see what Lisa was up against. Alex reminded me of Matt, only a 100 times more protective. Then again, Alex and Julie didn't have a mother watching over them.

What were their lives like? How could they endure without parents? How had Syl?

No matter how awful I'd had it, I realized how lucky I was. Even now, back in my freezing cold closet, the only light coming from my two flashlight pens, I do understand that, in spite of everything, I'm one of the lucky ones.

Chapter 9

June 3

If you'd asked me a week ago what it would take for me to feel better, I would've said knowing how Dad and Lisa and the baby were, meeting a boy my own age, and running water.

Now I have all three. I guess I must feel better.

Dad and Matt got the water running again, which, with ten people and a baby in the house, is a really good thing. All that snow and rain have finally paid off, and the sound of the toilets flushing is music to everybody's ears.

Gabriel isn't exactly Baby Rachel, but I think he's screaming a little bit less. Mom says Jon was colicky also, but I don't remember. Charlie is great with the baby. I think the only times Gabriel isn't crying is when he's nursing and when Charlie sings him lullabies.

Alex may not be the teenage boy of my dreams, but he is a teenage boy. He's eighteen, and if things had stayed normal, he'd be graduating high school this month and preparing to go to Georgetown. Julie told Jon, who told Mom, who told Matt, who told me.

If Alex isn't the teenage boy of my dreams, Julie seems to be the teenage girl of Jon's. Or maybe he's just as desperate for someone his age as I was. He and Julie always seem to be sitting next to each other and talking, even playing chess. I guess Alex approves of Jon and Mom approves of Julie. I know Mom approves of Alex, who stands up every time Mom enters a room and says please and thank you and may I help you. He's definitely Mom's dream of a teenage boy.

With all this happiness going on, you'd think I'd be happy, too. Or at least not as obsessed with how long the fish is going to last.

Except we all are. Nobody says so, because that would be rude. But today, instead of fish and a quarter can of vegetables each (except for Lisa, who gets double portions of everything), we had fish and a whiff of vegetables.

It's amazing. I never used to like red cabbage, but now when I get only a teaspoon of it, it's all I can think about. How lovely. How tasty. How <u>not</u> fish it is.

Pretty soon the fish is going to be not fish also.

Charlie eats the least of us, and I have to admit I thought he was sneaking into the garage and stealing shad until he told us a bit about himself.

"I used to weigh three hundred and seventy pounds," he told us over a quarter teaspoon of red cabbage. "I was scheduled for weight loss surgery on May twenty-third. Instead I went on a starvation diet, with lots of walking and biking for exercise." He laughed. "This is the best shape I've ever been in."

"It's an ill wind that doesn't blow anybody some good," Syl said, and we all stared at her.

"My grandmother used to say that," she said.

That got us laughing, and then we came up with clichés that used to mean something. The early bird catches the worm. Big fish in a small pond.

The best one was half a loaf is better than none at all. I thought we'd never stop laughing after Dad came up with that.

But then Gabriel started yowling, and Lisa nursed him for the 87th time that day and that quieted all of us.

"I've been thinking," Dad said. "It's been wonderful staying here, and Laura, you have no idea how grateful we are, but this house was never meant for ten people."

"I think we all know that," Mom said.

"Julie and I won't be staying much longer," Alex said. "We shouldn't have stayed as long as we have, but she needed the rest."

"You did, too," Julie said. "You're the one who collapsed last week."

"Julie," Alex said.

"We all needed the rest," Charlie said. "Laura, you—well, all of you have saved our lives."

"Alex and Julie have places to go to," Dad said. "But now that I have my children back, including Syl, who I didn't even know about before, I don't ever intend to leave you."

It's funny how relieved I felt when Dad said that. I'd been trying not to think of his going away again. Even though I'd know he and Lisa and Gabriel were alive, it would still be awful not to have them with me.

"The problem is we can't be sure you'll get any food," Matt said. "It took a fair amount of convincing before they'd give Syl any."

Dad nodded. "That's been my concern, too. We can't keep eating your food, and we can't be sure they'll give us some."

"But you're our father," I said. "That should count."

"Maybe for me," Dad said. "But there's Lisa to consider

and Charlie, and Alex and Julie for as long as we can get them to stay. I do have an idea, though, that might solve a lot of problems."

"Go on," Mom said.

"Mrs. Nesbitt's house is empty," Dad said. "But if her son came back, his family should be entitled to food. What was his name again?"

"Bobby," Mom said. "He lived in San Diego. Mrs. Nesbitt never heard from him . . ." She didn't finish the sentence. We never do. Some sentences don't need to be finished.

"Then no one knows if he's still alive," Dad said. "I'll go into town on Monday and say I'm Bob Nesbitt, that I brought my family back to see how Mom was doing, and we'll be moving into her house. Which we'll do anyway, since that way we won't be underfoot. It's me and my wife, what was her name?"

"Sally," Mom said.

"Me and Sally and our two kids, Alex and Julie, and the baby and my brother-in-law, Charlie. Who's going to know different?"

"Why should they believe you?" Matt asked. "I was there to vouch for Syl."

"Then I'll take one of you with me," Dad said. "Miranda? How would you feel about coming along and swearing I'm Bob Nesbitt?"

"Hal, I didn't bring up the kids to lie," Mom said.

"No," Dad said. "But you didn't bring them up to starve, either."

"I don't mind," I said, because I hated the thought of Mom and Dad going after each other. "If Syl's entitled, I don't see why Dad shouldn't be. And it would be great having everybody at Mrs. Nesbitt's."

"There's a woodstove in the kitchen," Matt said. "You'll need firewood. And some space heaters."

"We can look for those," I said. "And toilet paper and everything else they'll need. Oh, Mom, it'd be so great to have Dad there."

"Where's Mrs. Nesbitt's?" Alex asked, and Julie asked, "Who's Mrs. Nesbitt?" at the exact same time.

That got us laughing again. "She was our closest neighbor," Matt said. "Her house is right down the road. You can't see it from here, but there's a path through the woods we used to take."

"Then we're agreed?" Dad asked, although it wasn't exactly a question. "Miranda and I will go into town on Monday and see if they'll give us food. We'll spend the next few days here, until we can get set up at the Nesbitt house. Maybe if we can get food, we can convince Alex and Julie to stay a little longer."

"Please, Alex," Julie said.

"We'll see," Alex said.

Julie smiled, and suddenly I understood why Jon likes her so much. Her smile made you forget everything that's happened in the past year.

"We might as well give it a try," Mom said. "If Miranda is willing."

"I am, Mom," I said. But I don't think my smile made anyone forget anything.

June 4

I was in my bedroom, trying to decide what would be the absolutely safest place to hide my diaries, when I heard a knock on my door and Alex softly saying, "Miranda?"

Even though I hadn't touched a thing and my diaries

were as hidden as they ever are, I instantly decided I needed to find an even better place for them. That was after I finished jumping at the sound of a strange boy's voice.

"Yeah," I said, which didn't come off quite as friendly as it should have. "I mean, hi, Alex. What do you want?"

He stood in the doorway until I gestured for him to come in.

"I hope I'm not bothering you," he said. "I was wondering if you might have some clothes Julie could borrow. Just for the time we're here."

"Oh, sure," I said. "Julie's smaller than I am, but we can work something out." Syl already has half my wardrobe. Julie could have the other half.

"Thank you," he said. "It'll mean a lot to her."

"Do you want me to ask Matt if you could borrow some of his clothes?" I asked. Why should I be the only naked one in the house?

"That would be great, thank you," Alex said. "It's just for a few days, until Julie's rested up enough."

"There's no rush," I said. "I'll see what I can find."

Alex looked around my room. "You have a lot of books," he said.

"Not that many," I said. "And I've read all of them three times by now."

"I miss reading," he said, taking my copy of <u>Pride and Prejudice</u> off the shelf. "I miss learning useless things. Latin. Calculus."

"I miss friends," I said. "Friends. Family. Food. The three Fs." I smiled, but Alex didn't smile back.

"I miss home," he said. "And the feeling you got in a library carrel, like nothing in the world mattered except the book you were reading." He put <u>Pride and Prejudice</u> back on the shelf. "I miss pride. The sin of pride."

"I don't think it's a sin to be proud," I said, looking at my skating trophies. "Not if you've worked to achieve your goal."

Alex shook his head. "You don't understand," he said. "It's different for you. You work to keep your house clean, and you take pride in how it looks. That's not what I mean."

It annoyed me that Alex thought my only accomplishment in life was in the war against ash. "I take pride in lots of things," I said. "Like how my family has come together. How we've fought to keep alive. To keep our hopes alive. I take a lot of pride in that. Do you think that's a sin?"

"No, of course not," Alex said. "But that's not the kind of pride I'm talking about."

"Oh," I said. "You mean like vanity. Being proud because you're good-looking or rich."

"That's not it exactly, either," Alex said.

"Then what is it?" I asked.

He gazed out my window, at the perpetually gray landscape. "All right," he said. "Maybe you'll understand better if I tell you about the coin jar. We had to pay for our school uniforms, so my mother kept a coin jar. Every day we emptied our pockets and whatever change we had went into the jar. One day she caught my father taking out a handful of quarters. He was short on beer money. She went crazy. It was the worst fight I ever saw them have. My mother had ambitions for us. Every penny we saved was important to her." He paused for a moment. "My father picked up the coin jar and threw it across the room. The coins flew all over. My mother got down on her hands and knees to pick up the change, but my brother, Carlos, shoved me onto the floor. It was my fault, he said. I was the one they were fighting over."

"That must have been awful," I said. Mom and Dad at their worst always let us know we weren't to blame for their problems.

"I vowed I would never feel shame again," Alex said. "But the shame wasn't because my parents fought over me. It was the shame of crawling on the floor, sweeping pennies and nickels into a pile to pay for clothes other kids took for granted. The next day I got a job, started working wherever I could, finally got regular work at a pizza parlor. I paid for my own uniforms after that and my books, too. No more coin jar. My mother found some other way to pay for my sister's uniforms. And I felt proud. Proud I was smart. Proud that people noticed me, respected me. Proud that I was ambitious. Proud that I was too good to end up like my parents. And now I beg for clean clothes for my sister. I beg for every bite of food we eat."

"You don't have to beg here," I said. "We're happy to share."

"No one is happy to share," he said.

Alex looked down then or I looked up. I don't know how it happened, but we made eye contact, and for a moment I was drawn into his soul. I could see everything, the depth of his sorrow, his anger, his despair.

I feel sorrow and anger and despair. I don't think there's a person alive who doesn't. I sometimes feel like my sorrow and anger and despair burn inside me the way the sun used to burn on a hot July day.

But that was nothing compared to what I sensed in Alex. His sorrow, his anger, his despair was like a thousand suns, like a galaxy of suns. It physically hurt me to look into his eyes, but I couldn't break away. He turned his head first, and then he apologized, or maybe he thanked me. For Alex I think they're the same thing.

He bolted out of the room, leaving me to stare at my bookcase and think about the sin of pride and the sin of prejudice and all the other sins I'd left behind.

June 5

Dad and I biked into town today to talk to Mr. Danworth. I don't think I've ever seen Dad on a bike before, although I remember showing off to him when I rode a two-wheeler for the first time.

I'd thought it would be great having some time alone with Dad. We haven't had any since he got back, and there was so much I wanted to tell him and so much I wanted him to tell me. But the weather was awful. Not raining, but cold with a harsh wind blowing in our faces. March weather in June.

Maybe it was better we couldn't have a father/daughter talk, because by the time we got to City Hall to pick up our food and talk to Mr. Danworth, Dad was in full Bob Nesbitt mode.

"My wife and I didn't know what to expect," Dad said after he introduced himself. "Of course we hadn't heard from Mom, but you can't give up hope. And it is a miracle of sorts we're alive. Our home in San Diego is gone, but we were visiting Sally's brother, Charlie, when it all happened. There we were in Susanville. We would have stayed there, except for Mom. I was worried about her living on her own, with only Laura Evans and her kids looking in on her. So I convinced my wife and Charlie we needed to make our way east, and that turned out to be a miracle, too, since we were out of range of the volcanoes once they started erupting. Then on Christmas Day we had our third miracle when our baby, Gabriel, was born."

"How many in your family, did you say?" Mr. Danworth asked, which I figured was a good sign.

"Five, not including Gabriel," Dad said. "Although Sally needs extra food because she's nursing. There's Sally and me and our two older ones, Alex and Julie, and Sally's brother, Charlie. Alex and Julie are amazing kids, the best a father could dream of. Alex is so bright. Well, when all this is over with, I know he'll go on to college. And Julie's been a second mother to the baby. Every day I look at them and I thank God for all my blessings."

I felt really strange hearing Dad say all that. No, that's a lie. I didn't feel strange. I felt sick to my stomach. Not because I had to stand there and nod like it was all true, but because in a funny way it _is_ all true. Dad may have only known Alex and Julie for a couple of months, but there's a connectedness he doesn't have with us anymore. You can see it in the way he looks at them, the way he seems to absorb everything Alex says or the way he smiles at Julie. He's that way with Charlie, too. It's like they're all members of the same secret society, which no one else can join.

So when Mr. Danworth asked me if what Dad said was true and I said yes, it wasn't as much of a lie as it might have been. Not that I could ever explain that to Mom, or to anyone else. Jon wouldn't understand anyway, and Matt would understand a little too well.

"I suppose you folks are entitled to food," Mr. Danworth said. "Of course we can't give you any until next

Monday, so you're on your own till then. And I can't guarantee any for your brother-in-law or extra for your wife.
What we give you comes out of everybody else's. It's not like
we call the government and say there are five more people
in town so send us accordingly."

"Anything you can do," Dad said. "We'd be very grateful."

"Share and share alike," Mr. Danworth said, a cliché
that would have fit right in the other night. "Will you folks
be able to manage for another week?"

"We'll have to," Dad said. "You know how it is. We're
used to being hungry. As long as my wife has enough, we
can get by."

"A baby," Mr. Danworth said. "That truly is a miracle."

Dad grinned. "I wish I had pictures," he said. "Miranda,
isn't Gabriel the most beautiful baby you've ever seen?"

I started to say, "Yes, Dad," but I caught myself in time
and said, "Yes, definitely," instead. I know Dad caught it,
but Mr. Danworth didn't seem to notice.

"You know something?" Mr. Danworth said. "My wife
and I, well, we have a bit saved up. I'm going to give you my
bag, so your wife will have some for this week. A baby.
That's worth going hungry for."

"Thank you," Dad said. "You can't know what this
means to us."

"Maybe I'll come over one day and pay little Gabriel a
call," Mr. Danworth said.

"Any time," Dad said. "We'd be honored."

Dad and I talked a little bit on the ride home, since the
wind was to our backs. Not that I was in much of a mood—
although I was relieved about the extra food for Lisa. If
nothing else, it means the rest of us won't have to give up so
much of ours.

"When Lisa had the baby at the evac camp, people did that," Dad told me. "Not just Charlie. Lots of people. We had so little food, but people brought theirs for Lisa. Strangers who heard about the baby. It was so important to them that Lisa and Gabriel make it."

"If Gabriel had been a girl, what would you have named her?" I asked.

"Abigail," Dad said. "Abigail Hope Evans."

There went the last of my Baby Rachel fantasies.

"Someday you'll have children," Dad said. "You and Julie and Syl. God willing, I'll live to see that day."

"Maybe someday," I said. But the truth of the matter is when you spend your time thinking about your next meal and wanting your father to love you as much as he loves two strangers and trying to love your baby brother in spite of the fact that all he ever does is scream, it's hard to wish for a baby of your own.

Maybe someday.

Maybe not.

June 6

For the second time in a week the doorbell rang.

Everything was different this time. Matt, Dad, Alex, and Charlie were outside chopping trees. Jon and Julie were in the back of the sunroom. Julie's tutoring Jon in Spanish, which he's developed a mad desire to learn in the past couple of days. Syl was upstairs while Mom and Lisa were sitting cross-legged on the mattress, talking about what supplies Dad and Lisa could take to Mrs. Nesbitt's house. Gabriel was lying in his crib, taking it all in. And I was giving the kitchen a thorough cleaning, which is a lot easier with running water, even if the water is gray.

I looked out the kitchen window and saw Mr. Danworth standing at the back door. I was the farthest one away but the only one standing, so I walked over and let him in.

"I thought I'd pay a call on the baby," he said, which I knew meant "I thought I'd come over and make sure there really is a baby that I gave up a week of my food for."

"There he is," I said, pointing to the crib that used to be Mom's sweater drawer. "Gabriel, I'd like you to meet Mr. Danworth. He's in charge of feeding your mommy."

"Wow," Mr. Danworth said, bending for inspection. "What a big boy you are. He's quite the bruiser, isn't he." He turned around and saw Lisa. "You must be Sally Nesbitt," he said.

Lisa smiled. "Isn't he beautiful?" she said. "My Christmas miracle."

"Your husband mentioned he was born on Christmas," Mr. Danworth said. "Your family must have gone through a lot since then."

"Everyone has," Lisa said. "And we have Gabriel."

"He'll be crawling soon," Mr. Danworth said. "Getting ready to explore the world."

Lisa nodded. "He's going to make the world a better place," she said. "Not just for me, for all of us. He was born for a reason, I'm sure of it."

"That wouldn't surprise me one bit," Mr. Danworth said. He looked over our little domestic scene. "Hello, Laura," he said to Mom. "And Jon. Good to see you. Who's your friend, Jon?"

"I'm Julie," she told him. She hesitated so slightly I

may have been the only one to notice. "Dad and Alex and Uncle Charlie are outside," she said. "With Matt. If you want to talk with them."

"I'll give them a quick hello on my way out," Mr. Danworth said. "I can't get over this baby. Bob and Miranda told me all about him, but before I saw him with my own eyes, well, frankly I couldn't believe it. A baby here in Howell. It gives you faith."

"Would you like to hold him?" Lisa asked. "Gabriel's used to strangers. He won't mind."

"Can I?" Mr. Danworth asked. He bent down and picked Gabriel up. Gabriel, who still screeches at the sight of me, smiled at Mr. Danworth and tried to take his glasses off to play with.

Mom and Lisa and Julie were all beaming like Gabriel had pushed the moon back into place. Even Jon was grinning.

"You're quite the fella, aren't you," Mr. Danworth said. "You know, I could be holding the president of the United States in my arms right now. It wouldn't surprise me one bit."

Gabriel made some kind of gurgling noise in agreement, and everyone laughed. Well, everyone except me.

Because for the first time I really thought about Gabriel's future. If he exists, other babies must also. But how many of them will survive the next year, the next decade? I've had sixteen good years and one horrible one, but for Gabriel, for all the Gabriels, their whole lives will be like my one horrible year. Only I had the good years to see me through. What will they have?

And I finally figured out why Mom is willing to give up so much for her ex-husband's baby. Gabriel isn't just Dad's baby. He's Dad's future, Lisa's future. He's all our futures, even Mr. Danworth's. Every day Gabriel lives and grows a little bigger, a little stronger, is a miracle.

I stood there, and it's the stupidest thing, but tears started streaming down my face. It was Julie who walked over and gave me a hug.

"It's all right," she said. "You can love him, too."

Chapter 10

June 8

Mom is madly happy that Jon is interested in schoolwork, so she's taken over teaching him and Julie. Alex seems pleased that Julie's getting any kind of instruction, and with Dad and Charlie around, Jon isn't needed for the firewood anymore.

Mom asked both Syl and me if we wanted to join them, but neither one of us is interested in algebra. Lisa and Syl are doing Bible study, and in the evenings Dad and Charlie join them.

So I volunteered to get started on cleaning Mrs. Nesbitt's house. All that domesticity was getting on my nerves.

Cleaning Mrs. Nesbitt's is a big job, and tomorrow I'll ask for volunteers. But for one day I figured being alone would be nice. The plan is for Dad, Lisa, and Gabriel to sleep in the kitchen, since that's where the woodstove is, and Alex and Charlie will sleep in the parlor and Julie in the dining room. Then, when Alex and Julie leave, Charlie will move into the dining room, since that's warmer.

But now even Mom doesn't want Alex and Julie to go. She knows once they do, it'll be back to chopping wood for Jon, and she'll never be able to get him interested in schoolwork again. And I think she's hoping Alex's may-Is and thank-yous will rub off on me.

I don't know how I feel about them staying. It still hurts me to look at Dad looking at them, seeing the pride and love in his eyes. It's not like he looks at Matt or Jon or me any differently. Even Syl gets that same look. He loves all of us.

But he should love us more. He just should. We're his children, not Alex and Julie.

But then I see Alex and Julie together, talking quietly, playing chess, and I know that if people had seen Matt with Jon or me, pre-Syl Matt, that is, they would have fallen in love with us the way Dad has with Alex and Julie. If it had been Matt and Jon and me and we didn't have any parents, any family except each other, and people had reached out, included us in their families, it would have meant everything to us. It would have meant survival.

If I had to guess, I'd say Alex is going to move on, but he'll let Julie stay with Dad and Lisa. Lisa's counting on it, and now with Mom on her side I think the pressure will be too great for Alex. Especially with food coming in.

It wouldn't be too bad if Julie stayed. She wouldn't exactly be Baby Rachel, but I've adjusted to Syl, more or less. I could adjust to Julie.

Anyway, that's what I told myself as I cleaned Mrs. Nesbitt's kitchen and thought about how much my life has changed in just a single week.

June 9

I started out alone at Mrs. Nesbitt's, which I liked, since it gave me more of a chance to feel sorry for myself. Just call me Cinderella Evans.

But then the wicked stepsisters (Syl and Julie) came over to help clean, which I don't remember happening in Cinderella. What made it even worse is they're both dynamos. When you're alone in a freezing cold house, mopping and moping, you can take your time. But when there are two other people and they're actually working, you have to pick up your pace and accomplish something.

So I was relieved when Alex showed up about an hour later. "I thought I'd go scavenge houses," he said. "Miranda, would you mind coming along? You know the area and I don't."

Mind? Breaking into houses with the last living boy in America I'm not related to versus scrubbing every inch of a kitchen floor?

"No, that's okay. I'll go," I said.

"Good," Alex said. "Thank you."

When other people say things like that, simple things like "good" and "thank you," they smile. Alex didn't smile. Alex never smiles. He says "please" and "thank you" and "may I," but he never smiles.

I wonder if he used to before.

We went back to the house, told Mom where we were going, got bags and bikes, and rode off, leaving Syl and Julie to clean and polish. Alex may not have smiled, but I sure did.

"I've been going to houses closer to town," I told him as we began. "More suburby places, lots of houses near each other. I've been doing pretty well there."

"Let's try more isolated," Alex said. "Farmhouses. Cabins in the woods."

That annoyed me. He asked me along since I know the area. Then he rejected my suggestion about where to look.

I have a big brother, thank you. I don't need the last living boy in America to treat me like a dumb kid sister.

"We'll do better in the suburbs," I said.

"How do you know?" he asked. "If you haven't tried the country?"

For a moment I considered turning around and going back to Mrs. Nesbitt's. Let Alex get lost on his own, since he was so determined to bike vast distances for no good reason whatsoever.

But it's the middle of June, the temperature had to be close to sixty, and if you really concentrated, you could kind of make out the sun. And even if Alex was the most annoying, last living boy in America, he still was the last living boy in America. (I should come up with initials for that: LLBA or something.)

"All right," I said. "You want country, we'll try country." I began biking a little faster than him, taking the lead. We rode along at a steady pace while I tried to decide how far we should go to satisfy him.

I'd like to say I didn't know where we were going, but that wouldn't be true. I had a flash of "I'll show him" when I turned onto Hadder's Road, and then made the left onto Murray, the back road to the high school.

We were there in fifteen minutes. The mound of bodies. Only in the month since I'd been there, the temperature's gone above freezing, the snow has melted, and the bodies have started to decompose.

It was awful. The stench was unbearable, even outdoors. The bodies were bloated, the faces unrecognizable. As bad as my nightmares have been, the reality is far worse. And it had been my choice to go there, to punish Alex for going against my advice.

"I wondered where all the bodies were," he said like he wondered where Mom hid the Christmas presents.

"I know people there," I said. "Friends of mine are in that pile."

Alex stopped his bike and bowed his head in prayer, which made me feel even worse. Especially since the sight and the smell sickened me and all I wanted to do was get as far away as possible.

"It's hard to lose friends," he said.

I figured that meant we could start biking again. "Have you lost friends, too?" I asked.

"Everyone has," he said.

I thought that was a pretty lousy answer. He could have consoled me for my losses or he could have told me about his, but to point out the whole world is a rotten stinking mass of death didn't make me feel any better.

And I resent being told the whole world is a rotten stinking mass of death. Every night Mom turns on the radio and gets stations from Pittsburgh and Nashville and Atlanta, and we get to hear, every single night, about their rotten stinking masses of death.

So I didn't need Alex to point out that everyone on earth has lost friends.

The one good thing about getting mad was it made me bike even faster. This time, though, I paid attention to where we made our turns and what roads we were on. I had no desire to get lost with this particular LLBA.

One of us would spot a farmhouse, and we'd check it for signs of life—more carefully than I had in the past because it's warmer and there's a chance people inside weren't using their woodstoves. But the first three we went to were empty. The only problem was they were empty inside as well. We took half a bar of soap and a quarter tube of toothpaste and not much more.

I considered resisting saying "I told you so" but gave in to the temptation. "I didn't think we'd do so well out here," I said. "People in the country stayed on longer, so they used up all their stuff."

"You never know," he said, which I took to mean "Shut up, you stupid girl."

I wonder what Cinderella would have done with a wicked stepbrother.

We did better with house number four: a summer cabin you couldn't see from the road. Most likely no one had used it the year before, so whatever was there was two years old. But that doesn't matter when it comes to soap and paper towels. And because it was a summer house, there was lots of summer house reading. I grabbed a dozen paperback mysteries for Mom and some romances for Lisa and Syl.

"I'm sorry there are no Latin books for you," I said.

"I'm sorry we can't eat books," he said.

If Alex knew how to smile, maybe he would have smiled then, and I would have known it was a joke and smiled back. But he doesn't and he didn't and I didn't.

We kept biking up that road, stopping at a couple more cabins, but mostly finding more of the same. One house, miraculously, had a half box of disposable diapers. Syl and I have been the diaper service since Gabriel's arrival, and even a dozen disposables looked like treasure.

Our trash bags still looked empty, so we kept on. The houses were getting more isolated, and I was glad to have Alex by my side as we searched.

I can't say the last house we went to was going to be the last one of the day. Alex hadn't said we should stop looking, and every half roll of toilet paper will make our lives a little bit better. Maybe we would have kept on for another hour or two.

And neither one of us noticed anything particularly different about the final house we went to. I could tell right away it wasn't a summer house, but that didn't mean anything.

We used Alex's trick of throwing a few pebbles against a door and then running for cover in case anybody started shooting. No one did, so we got closer and looked through the windows for signs of life. When we thought it was safe, we tried the doors, which were locked, and threw a stone through the living room window.

The sound of shattering glass has replaced doorbells in my life.

It was Alex's turn to stick his hand through the window and unlock it. I love breaking in, but that's my least favorite part, since there's a part of me that's sure whoever owns the house is waiting to chop off my hand. I've had lots of nightmares about that.

But no one came at us with an ax, so we climbed in.

We both smelled death right away. It was like the mound of bodies only worse because the house was all closed up and the smell had intensified.

"Please," I said. "Let's go."

"Wait outside if you want," Alex said.

But I knew what I didn't see would frighten me more than what I did. "I'll be okay," I said. I've told bigger lies.

Alex took my hand. I could see his was bleeding. "You cut yourself," I said to hide the fact that I was shaking from fear and excitement at the touch of a boy's hand.

"Just a scratch," he said, but he pulled his hand from mine. "I'm sorry. I didn't mean to get blood on you."

I nodded. Alex began walking toward the smell and I followed him.

The body was in the kitchen. Once it had been human, sitting in the chair next to where we found it. Or what remained of it, some torn clothing, a belt, some flesh and muscle, hair, bones, an eyeball. By its side was a shotgun, and lying a few feet away was a dead pit bull.

I screamed.

"Don't look," Alex said, but I couldn't avert my eyes. He walked around the corpse, took a red plaid vinyl tablecloth and flung it on top. Then he held me until I stopped shaking.

"I think we're in luck," he said. "The dog died recently, maybe even today. It's been eating its owner for a while now, but it finally starved to death. There's probably dog food if we look."

"I don't know if Horton will eat dog food," I said.

"Not for Horton," Alex said. "For us." He began searching through the kitchen cabinets. Sure enough, there were a couple of cans. Dinner, I thought, grateful that Alex hadn't suggested we eat the dog.

"All right?" I asked, my voice sounding squeaky even to me. "Can we go now?"

"There's more," Alex said. "Can't you sense it? He was protecting more than two cans of dog food."

"But he's dead," I said. "Maybe he killed himself when he ran out of food."

"Maybe," Alex said. "But we should look around anyway. For toilet paper and diapers."

We both knew there weren't going to be any diapers, but I was just as happy to get out of the kitchen. We went through the house thoroughly, taking anything we could use, which wasn't very much. Alex even went down to the cellar but came back empty-handed.

"I guess your hunch was wrong," I said.

"I still feel it," he said. "He would have shot his dog first if he was going to kill himself. He loved that dog."

I knew Alex was right, because if it came to that for us, we would have killed Horton or at least let him loose. "There's a garage," I said. "Maybe there's something out there."

"Then he would have been sitting in the garage with his shotgun," Alex said. "It's in the house somewhere. We're overlooking something."

"It could be money," I said. "Or jewelry. Things he thought were valuable."

Alex shook his head. "The dog just died," he said for the third time, like he was Sherlock Holmes and I was the world's stupidest Dr. Watson. "He ate off the man for a few days and then went a few days without eating. This guy, whoever he is, died fairly recently. He knew what was valuable."

"All right," I said. "Where, then? We've looked everywhere."

"Not in the attic," Alex said. "Wouldn't this house have an attic?"

"At least a crawlspace," I said. "But I didn't see a staircase. Maybe there's a trapdoor."

We went upstairs and looked through three closets before finding the trapdoor to the attic. Alex pulled on the cord, and I climbed the stairs.

There were cartons everywhere. But cartons in an attic mean nothing. Even cartons that had the names of products mean nothing. Even cartons still sealed mean nothing.

Alex followed me up. The roof was so low neither one of us could stand upright. There wasn't much space to walk anyway, but we could move around well enough for him to pull out a penknife and cut open a Campbell's Chicken Noodle Soup carton.

Inside it were twenty-four cans of Campbell's Chicken Noodle Soup.

"He didn't starve to death," I said. "How could he with all this food?"

"He was a miser," Alex said. "You'd hear about guys like that, but I always thought they were folktales. People who stocked up when it first happened and then were so afraid of not having enough, they stopped eating what they had. You stay here. I'll be back up in a moment."

I had no idea why he was leaving but I didn't care. I looked at box after glorious box. Some of the food, I knew, had gone rotten. But there was still so much. Even with ten of us there was enough food for weeks.

When Alex came back up, he had the man's shotgun. "Just in case we need it," he said.

"How can we get all this back home?" I asked, hoping Alex knew how to handle a shotgun. "Maybe we should move here until the food runs out."

"The house is too small," Alex said. "Besides, a guy like that had to have some way of getting out. He'll have a van in the garage, or a pickup, with a little gas in the tank. Enough to get the food back to your house. I bet he has some containers as well. He was prepared. Crazy but prepared."

"What if the garage is locked?" I asked.

"It probably is," Alex said. "But there was a key ring on the guy's belt."

I remembered what the man looked like and shuddered. Not a cute, little horror movie shiver, either.

"It's okay," Alex said. "It's a lot to take in. I'll get the key and check out the garage. You stay here. It'll be all right." He took the shotgun with him and climbed down the stairs.

I forced myself to read the cartons, to concentrate on the miracle of black beans and beef jerky. The sight of four 20-pound bags of rice thrilled me. But I was never more relieved than when I heard Alex enter the closet.

"It's a van," he said. "With a quarter tank of gas. I found a couple cans of gas, too." He shook his head. "He could have gone anywhere with two cans of gas," he said. "He and the dog both."

"Is it stick shift?" I asked. "I don't know how to drive stick shift."

"I know how," Alex said. "You learn things on the road. How to drive. How to hot-wire. How to defend yourself." He paused for a moment. "You'd be amazed how many cars there are with a little bit of gas left in them. You hot-wire a car and you can go twenty-five miles on fumes."

"That's how you got here?" I asked. "Dad and Lisa and Charlie, too? By car?"

"Some," Alex said. "Some we biked and some we walked. Julie and I got a lift partway to Tulsa in February. That was a big help. Then we left Tulsa to find Carlos in Texas. His Marine regiment is stationed there. By the time we located him, we knew everything we needed to survive."

I knew I'd ask about Tulsa later, but the important thing was getting all the food back home. "I had an idea,"

I said. "See that window? I could toss the cartons to the ground. They're cans and boxes, so nothing would break."

"Great idea," Alex said. "You stay here and do the tossing. I'll go down, and when you're through, we'll load the van."

At first I resented the idea that I'd do all the heavy lifting, but then I realized Alex would be outside with the shotgun. He and Julie knew how to defend themselves, but no one had bothered to teach me. "Fair enough," I said.

We shattered open the window, and Alex watched as I threw a box down. "Good work," he said. He picked up one of the bags of rice and carried it down while I kept tossing the boxes out the window. A couple of them flew open, but mostly they held.

It took a while for me to get them all down, and I was exhausted by the time I'd finished, but the job was only partly done. We still had to get three bags of rice outside, and we couldn't toss them. Alex came back, and we each took one. I had no idea how heavy twenty pounds could be. Alex handed me the shotgun, then went to the attic and got the final bag.

The van looked really old, and its windows had been whitewashed so you couldn't see in. But it held everything, except our bikes. Those Alex and I strapped to the top with rope he'd found.

The sound of the engine turning over was just amazing. The sensation of being in a van that actually moved was beyond description.

"Do you know how to get back?" I asked. "Or should I direct?"

"I'll need your directions," Alex said. "I try to remember landmarks, but this country all looks the same to me."

So I told him where to turn. There were no other cars on the road, and no one came out at the sound of ours. I was relieved, since Alex had given me the shotgun and I was terrified I'd be expected to use it.

"Who was in Tulsa?" I asked. "Or did you just pass through there?" It was easier to ask Alex questions with us both facing forward with no danger of eye contact.

"We thought we'd find our aunt and uncle," Alex said. "They set out for there last June. We spent a few days looking but no luck."

"It's hard to picture cities," I said. "Cities with people."

"They're not like before," Alex said. "There are bodies, mostly skeletons now, piled up. Even the rats have died. And only some buildings have heat, so you share apartments."

"Are there schools?" I asked, remembering my idea about places for politicians and millionaires to live. "Hospitals? Could you and Julie have stayed there?"

Alex held on to the steering wheel a little tighter. "The plan was for me to leave Julie with our aunt and uncle. I was going to get to Texas, find Carlos, let him know where we were, and then go back and work at the oil fields. But I couldn't leave Julie alone, so we went to Texas together."

"But you didn't stay," I said. "Couldn't you have worked in the Texas oil fields instead?"

"I could have," Alex replied. "But there was no one to look after Julie."

"Julie's a good kid," I said. "She wouldn't have gotten into trouble."

"Trouble would have found her," Alex said. "We couldn't take that risk."

I considered asking him about the convent, but I didn't

want to remind Alex that he'd caught me eavesdropping. "Could Dad and Lisa have stayed?" I asked instead. "Not necessarily in Tulsa. But in a city somewhere? Could Dad have gotten work?"

"Maybe," Alex said. "Maybe not. It's all physical labor. But the only thing that mattered to him, besides Lisa and the baby, was getting home to you. He talked so much about you, I felt like I knew you before we ever met. You were on your swim team, and before that you used to figure skate, and you played Glinda the Good in your fourth grade play."

"He told you all that?" I asked.

"And more," Alex said. "About all of you."

I thought about Dad, about how I'd even for a moment thought he could love anyone like he loves us, and I felt happy and guilty at the same time. But mostly I felt grateful to Alex, even though there was no way he could know how much his comment meant to me.

"Can I ask you a question now?" he said.

"Absolutely," I said. LLBA was asking _me_ a question.

"The bruises on your face," he said. "When we got here a week ago, they were pretty bad. How did you get them?"

It's nice to know the first thing he'd noticed about me was my ravishing collection of black-and-blue marks. "I took a header off my bike," I said.

"Oh," he said. "Julie and I had a bet going."

"Who won?" I asked, trying to keep the irritation out of my voice.

"We both lost," Alex said. "Her money was on you and Syl having a fight. Mine was on Matt slugging you one."

"Matt's never hit me," I said. "We weren't brought up like that, like animals."

"Neither were we," Alex said. "You don't have to be an animal to hit your sister."

"Not in my household," I said, sounding exactly like Mom.

"Fine," Alex said, sounding exactly like me.

We drove the rest of the way in silence, except for when I told him to make a turn. But it was hard for me to stay sulky when I was so excited about all the food we were bringing back in our very own van with its very own containers of gas.

Mom and Lisa stayed inside, trying to find places for all the cartons, while the rest of us carried in the food. The excitement was contagious. Charlie sang "Oh, What a Beautiful Mornin'," and Julie danced around, and Matt and Syl grabbed each other, and Dad cried with joy.

And I discovered that Alex knows how to smile.

June 10

You'd think with a houseful of food for the first time in a year, we'd be eating nonstop. Oh no. Not us.

First off, Matt pointed out that what seems like an enormous amount of food now is going to vanish in the blink of an eye with ten people eating it. Okay, he didn't say "in the blink of an eye." He said that if we each ate four ounces of rice a day, we'd finish the four twenty-pound bags in a month.

Four ounces of rice sounds like a lot of rice to me. And there's all that other food we brought back, plus the food we get each week, plus whatever shad is still in the garage. But Mom agreed with Matt that we'd have to be very careful to stretch out our supplies for a long time.

Then Charlie—Mr. Oh, What a Beautiful Mornin'—

pointed out that some of the food might have spoiled, and it would be a disaster if we came down with food poisoning at the same time.

He suggested we become food buddies (that was his exact term, "food buddies"), and every morning two of us could take a nibble from one kind of food and two of us from another, etc., and then if we didn't get sick, we could all eat the food we'd started that morning.

Matt and Syl said they'd be food buddies, and Jon volunteered himself and Julie, which left Alex and me. Dad and Charlie said they'd food-buddy, also, and we agreed Mom and Lisa shouldn't risk it.

This morning Alex and I each had a bite of canned mushrooms, and Jon and Julie had a bite of beef jerky, and Matt and Syl had a bite of canned carrots, and Dad and Charlie had a sip of vegetable soup.

We're all still alive.

And none of us have yet eaten our four ounces of rice.

June 11

My food buddy and I ate a bite of spinach this morning. I don't like spinach and I'm not at all sure I like Alex.

It's Sunday, so after breakfast Alex and Julie went off to the dining room and prayed there while Dad, Lisa, Charlie, Syl, and Matt prayed in the sunroom.

Jon looked conflicted about which group to join but ended up in the dining room with Alex and Julie. I guess he figured since he sleeps in the dining room, it was okay to be there.

I'm not feeling real religious these days and Mom never has, so we chose to organize our fabulous food supply, one cabinet for food that hasn't killed us and another for food we're going to try next and another for food we get from town. We also separated all the food with expiration dates from over a year ago. We didn't throw it out, because who knows how desperate we might get when we run out of rice, but we tucked it away where it wouldn't tempt us.

All this while Charlie and Lisa and Syl and Dad sang hymns. Matt kind of hummed along.

Eventually Gabriel decided to blow his horn, which broke up the sunroom revival meeting. The dining room Catholics (and potential convert) lasted a little longer.

While Mom and I flattened the cartons, we gave thanks, in our own way, for the merciful bounty that's come our way.

Chapter 11

June 12

Jon and Julie biked into town to get our Monday food. Julie offered to drive the van, and Mom nearly had a fit.

When they got back, they were loaded with a dozen bags of food.

"One bag for each of us," Julie said. "Including Gabriel. And an extra bag for Lisa."

There was less in each bag than we used to get, but it was still very nice of them to include extra for Lisa and to throw in a bag for Gabriel. With all the food in the house and none of it poisoning us so far, the food from town is pretty much a supplement.

Amazing. Enough food for all of us.

"I don't know how we're going to do it," Mom said. "But let's have a feast tonight."

"Like a party?" Julie asked.

"Exactly like a party," Mom said. "Lisa, is it all right with you if we have a party in the sunroom?"

"It's a wonderful idea," Lisa said. "Why don't we move our mattresses into the dining room and spread blankets out, like a picnic."

"Miranda, go tell the guys they need to come in early tonight," Mom said. "Alex, too, of course. Julie, you go upstairs and tell Syl."

"A party," Dad said when I told him. "Great idea. We have a lot to celebrate. Matt's marriage, and our homecoming, and the food, and our move to Mrs. Nesbitt's."

Matt didn't look all that excited, and Alex looked uncomfortable, but Dad didn't notice. Dad always liked parties.

Charlie, Syl, and I lugged Dad and Lisa's mattresses into the dining room. Lisa took Gabriel into the kitchen with her while I gave the sunroom floor a good mopping. Julie and Charlie went to Mrs. Nesbitt's to get her silverware and glasses. We've been eating in shifts, so we never needed service for ten.

Since we've gone three days without food poisoning, we had a lot of opened cans to eat from. Plus rice and shad.

The electricity cooperated by staying on almost all evening, so in addition to cooking on the woodstove, we used the microwave. There was no way we could cook enough for ten people at one time. So first we had a few sips of vegetable soup, and then we shared bites of spinach and mushrooms, and then the main course of rice, shad, and green beans. We each had two dried figs for dessert.

Then the party began. We're used to spending the evenings together in the sunroom, Bible studies in one corner, chess and card games in another, but the whole idea of a party is to play the same games together. Charlie suggested charades.

"What's charades?" Julie asked.

I had the feeling Alex didn't know, either, but to be fair about it, I doubt Jon does and it's not like I've ever played.

Charlie explained about acting out names of songs or movies or books, and we divided into boys vs. girls. The boys went into the kitchen to come up with their titles, and we girls stayed in the sunroom to work out ours. Gabriel was an honorary girl. Mom sacrificed a piece of typing paper for us to write our titles on, and Jon donated the use of his Phillies cap for the girls' slips of paper and his Yankees cap for the boys'. Then Charlie coached all of us on how to divide words into syllables and to cup your ear for "sounds like."

It turned out to be hard coming up with names of things. You want something that's perfect to stump the other team, but it's not like I've seen a lot of movies lately or read a lot of books. And all the songs seemed too obvious. But we each came up with two names, put them in the cap, and played.

Alex went first, and he pulled out Mom's choice of <u>Little Women</u>, which was much too easy. Lisa went next, and she got Matt's title, <u>Finnegans Wake</u>, which was impossible, even though Mom said she had tried to read it once.

But it didn't matter, because whether we did well (Dad and Syl were the best at acting things out, and Mom was the best at guessing) or miserably (Jon, with me a close second), it was a lot of fun. It feels like such a long time since I've done anything silly. At least intentionally silly.

We played until the electricity went off, but we were still enjoying ourselves, so Syl ran upstairs and got Matt's old guitar.

"I've been teaching myself," Syl said. "I'm not very good yet."

She had to be better than Matt, though. He got the guitar for his fourteenth birthday, played it nonstop for three days, and never looked at it again.

Syl strummed chords and Charlie sang, and then we all sang. Julie, it turns out, has a pretty voice, and with candles and the woodstove for light, you could see Alex's face glowing with pride. Which made me kind of like him again, at least for a minute or two.

After we'd finished massacring every Beatles song we could remember any of the words to, Charlie said to Syl, "I'd like to learn how to play the guitar. My fingers were always too fat before. Would you mind if I learned with you?"

"Not at all," Syl said. "That would be fun."

"I'd like to learn, too," Julie said. "Could we start tomorrow?"

"There's no point," Alex said. "We'll be leaving in a day or two."

"I don't want to go," Julie said. "I want to stay with Hal and Lisa and Gabriel." She paused for a moment. "And Charlie, too," she said. "And Jon."

"We've stayed too long as it is," Alex said. "You know what the plan is, Julie. It's not open for discussion."

"It's not fair!" Julie yelled. "No one asked me what I want to do!"

I'd write what Alex yelled back at her, but he switched to Spanish. I didn't understand what they were saying, but there was no doubting the tone.

Matt and I have had our fights, but we never sounded that bad. The fights we had were over hogging the computer or getting in each other's way. He was mean. I was a pest. We had fights like that with Jon, too.

But this, whatever it was they were saying, was much deeper, much angrier. I guess it was the fight brothers and sisters have when they don't have parents to stop them.

For a moment I was afraid Alex might hit Julie, but that was just in my head, since he didn't step any closer to her. But he must have said something really bad and Julie must have said something even worse because she ran outside, slamming the door behind her.

"She'll freeze out there," Lisa said.

"No," Alex said. "She'll be all right. Let her cool off."

He had to have felt all of us staring at him. "I'm sorry," he said. "She doesn't want to leave. But it's the right thing."

"Is it?" Dad asked. "You know how much we love Julie. She's family. She'll be safe with us."

Alex shook his head. "I know you mean that, Hal, and I'm grateful. But there's food now and it feels safe. Things change too fast."

"Even if we left, we'd take her with us," Dad said. "She'll always have a home with us."

"If you have a home," Alex said. "For as long as you have food. No, the decision's been made, and it's the right one, even if Julie doesn't see that. No matter what happens, we trust the church to protect her."

Which was more than Alex was doing, letting her run outside without a coat. I got up, grabbed one, and carried it outside.

Julie was standing by the garage, close to where I'd been the night Mom kicked me out. Only it was raining that night, so I got to suffer more. I grinned at winning the martyr contest.

"I brought you this," I said, handing Julie the coat.

"Thank you," she said, putting it on. "What's Alex doing? Explaining how wonderful the church is?"

"Pretty much," I said. "Would you rather stay with us? Even if Alex goes?"

"Yeah," Julie said. "But he won't let me. Carlos said I had to go to the convent. We told him about it, and he couldn't find anyplace else for me to stay, so he said I had to go there. I told him I didn't want to, but he said I had to anyway. And Alex said Carlos was right."

"It's a shame you couldn't find your aunt and uncle," I said. "Alex told me about them, how you could have stayed there while he worked in the oil fields."

"We didn't want to live in Tulsa," Julie replied. "I'd have been stuck taking care of my cousins. You think Gabriel cries a lot? He's nothing compared to them. And Alex'll be much happier in a monastery than he would be in an oil field."

"Monastery?" I said. I don't think I've ever said that word before. "Alex wants to enter a monastery?"

"Didn't he tell you?" Julie asked. "I thought Alex told you everything. I thought maybe he'd like you so much, he'd change his mind."

I almost burst out laughing. The last living boy in America drops into my bedroom only he wants to be a monk. I think that pretty much sums up my life.

"He doesn't like me that much," I said. "And he never told me."

"It isn't what he used to want," Julie said. "Before. He wanted to be president of the United States. And I bet he could have been. He's so smart and he worked all the time. But after we left Carlos, Alex said he'd take me to the convent and then he'd enter a monastery. There's a Franciscan one in Ohio that's still open. I'm never going to be a nun, though. I'll stay as long as I have to and then I'll come back here. If you're gone, I'll try to find you."

"We won't be going anytime soon," I said. "Mom

doesn't want us to leave, and since Dad and Lisa and the baby can stay at Mrs. Nesbitt's, there's no reason for them to go, either."

"People leave," Julie said.

I knew she was right, even though I couldn't picture us leaving anytime soon. "If we do go, we'll let you know," I said. "I promise you that."

"And I promise you, you're going to freeze without a coat," Charlie said, approaching us. "It may be the middle of June, but it's freezing out here."

"Not freezing," I said, gratefully taking my coat from him. "It's definitely above freezing."

"You're right," Charlie said. "It's got to be at least forty." He laughed. "I used to hate hot weather," he said. "Just breathing made me sweat. But now I think about hot summer nights and everything I would give up for one."

"What?" Julie said. "What would you give up?"

Charlie laughed again. "I don't know," he said. "Not any of you and I don't have anything else. I guess I don't have anything to barter."

"I used to think there'd still be stars in the sky," Julie said. "In the country, I mean. We used to spend summers in the country with Fresh Air Fund families, and there were always stars. I had a postcard once of a painting with big crazy-looking stars."

"<u>Starry Night</u>," I said. "Vincent van Gogh painted it. I saw it in a museum in New York. You're from New York, aren't you, Julie? Did you ever see it?"

"No," Julie said. "But I've been to museums. I went on a school trip to the Natural History Museum once. We looked at the dinosaurs for hours."

"The dinosaurs are gone," I said. "Just like the stars."

"The stars are there," Charlie said. "Hiding behind the ash clouds, but they're still there."

"I don't believe in anything I can't see," I said.

"You don't have to see God to believe in Him," Julie said. "You can feel Him and la Santa Madre and the saints. Like you can feel the sun, even though we can't see it anymore."

"I can't see the stars and I certainly can't feel them, so I've given up believing they're there," I said. "As far as I'm concerned, they no longer exist."

"Look at it this way," Charlie said. "Do you think there's life on other planets?"

"Yeah," I said. "And I hope they're having a better time of it than we are."

Charlie laughed. "Okay, then," he said. "Picture Princess Leia on her planet, or a Klingon, or some eight-eyed thing with four brains. And whatever it is, it's outside on a hot June night, looking at the ten thousand stars in its sky. Our sun is one of them. It can see our sun better than we can, and it has a name for it, like we have names for the stars. But Princess Leia doesn't know we're standing here looking up to where the stars used to be. Does that mean we don't exist just because she can't see us?"

I had never thought about that before: all the life on all the other planets throughout the universe as unaware of our lives, our suffering, as we are of theirs.

I wondered how many teenage boys there were out there and how many of them planned on becoming monks, and I laughed.

Charlie laughed with me and Julie did also. We were probably all laughing at different things, but that was okay. We were alive, we were together, and somewhere in the June sky there were stars.

Moving day.

Naturally it poured.

Mom stayed in and watched over Gabriel while the rest of us lugged stuff over to Mrs. Nesbitt's. Food, blankets, sheets, the clothes we've been sharing with everyone else. Lots of books.

I didn't believe it until Dad came back for Gabriel. But they really are gone. Even if it's just down the road.

There are only five us now, and it's so quiet.

Chapter 12

Lisa came over this morning, distraught.

"Alex says he's taking Julie away tomorrow," she said. "Miranda, you're the only one he listens to. Please talk to him."

I don't know where people have gotten the idea that Alex listens to me. Matt listens to Syl and Jon listens to Julie, but that seems to be where the listening ends.

Still, I told Lisa I'd give it a try.

I walked outside to where the guys were chopping wood. "I was wondering if I could borrow Alex for a few hours," I said, nice and casually. "I'd like to do some house hunting, and Mom doesn't like me to go alone."

"Good idea," Matt said. "Alex, you don't mind, do you? You and Miranda had great luck last time."

"Sure," Alex said. I get the feeling chopping wood is one thing he isn't going to miss at the monastery.

We walked back to the houses and got our bikes. It was as warm a day as I could remember, almost muggy, and we biked slowly.

"No country this time," I said. "Let's do Fresh Meadows instead."

"All right," Alex said.

Well, that was easy. Maybe he was in an agreeable mood. Or maybe he didn't like looking at half-eaten bodies any more than I did.

When I was a kid, I used to fantasize about living in Fresh Meadows. It's at the other end of town from us, five or six miles away, and it's where the doctors and lawyers live. Or lived before everything happened.

"These are nice houses," Alex said as we climbed our way through an already shattered window. "The rich kids lived here, huh?"

"No one was rich in Howell," I said. "But the richer kids lived here."

"I like your house better," Alex said. "It reminds me of home. All the people stepping over each other. We were pretty crowded."

I pictured Alex and Julie and Carlos living in a filthy tenement, with everybody yelling in Spanish and hitting each other. "Where was that?" I asked.

"West End Avenue and Eighty-eighth Street," Alex said.

There went my tenement fantasy. Actually, there went most of my ideas about Alex and Julie and where they came from. It costs a lot more money to live on West End Avenue and Eighty-eighth Street than it does to live in Fresh Meadows.

I guess Alex sensed my surprise. "My father was the super," he said. "Not much salary, but they let us live in the basement apartment, by the laundry room and the furnace."

"Oh," I said. "No wonder our house reminds you of home."

Alex laughed. "It's better than I made it sound," he said. "It was a nice apartment. But crowded and noisy."

We walked through the house together, taking whatever pickings we could find. I taught Alex the cosmetic bag trick, and he admired the travel-sized shampoos and soaps. We went through three houses that way, all of them previously ransacked, probably more than once. But each had a little something we could use, and we both enjoyed the quiet and the nice furnishings.

"No food today," I said. "No misers in this neighborhood."

"No," Alex said. "The rich don't starve."

"Are there special places for rich people, do you think?" I asked. "Did you ever see any?"

"There are safe towns," Alex said. "But they're hidden. Even Carlos couldn't find one."

Syl had mentioned trucks going to safe towns. Truckers must know where they were located even if the Marines didn't.

"We're safe enough where we are," I said. "We have food and shelter. Julie would be safe, too, if you let her stay with us."

"No," Alex said. "We're leaving tomorrow."

"But why?" I cried. "Charlie's staying. He's no more a part of the family than you are."

"Did you hear yourself?" Alex asked. "That's exactly why Julie has to go. No matter how much you say you love her, she isn't a part of your family. She's Carlos's sister and mine, not yours."

"Carlos isn't here," I said. "We are. You could be, too. You could both stay with us."

"No," Alex said. "Carlos told us what we should do, and we're doing it."

"You really will make a great monk," I said. "You have the obedience thing down pat."

"I have no idea what kind of monk I'll be," Alex said. "Or even if the order will take me in."

"Wait a second," I said. "You're dumping Julie with some nuns and then you're going to Ohio on the off chance you can become a monk? Are you serious?"

"That's exactly why I didn't tell you," Alex said. "I knew you wouldn't understand."

"That's not fair," I said. "Maybe I don't understand, but you didn't know if I would. You may know Latin and calculus and how to hot-wire a car, but you don't know anything about me. I don't think you know anything about anybody except yourself."

Alex looked around at what had once been a very nice living room, now covered with ash and broken glass. "I'll tell you what I know," he said. "Everywhere there's death. You think that pile of bodies was the worst thing I've ever seen? Or the corpse with the dog beside it? That was nothing. Every day for a year I've seen worse. I spent a lot of time trying to figure out why God lets me live when so many people have died horrible, lonely deaths. People better than I'll ever be. For a long time I thought I was alive to protect Julie, but every plan I've made for her failed. Now I'm trusting in Carlos's decision. And if God shows us mercy and gives Julie the protection I can't, I'll go to Ohio and beg the Franciscans to take me in and devote the rest of my life to serving Christ and my church. That's everything I know, Miranda. Everything."

He was crying. For days I hadn't known he could smile, and now I found he could cry.

"Stay until Tuesday," I said. "Go into town and get the food. Do that for Dad and Lisa, all right?"

He took a deep breath and wiped the tears off his cheeks. "Tuesday," he said. "What's today?"

"I'm not sure," I admitted, but then I counted back to last Monday. That's how we tell time: Monday to Monday. "It's Thursday," I said. "That's just a long weekend."

"All right," he said. "We'll leave on Tuesday. No more arguments."

"None," I said, but I felt a glimmer of hope.

Maybe Alex really does listen to me.

June 16

I opened one of the cans of dog food and put some in Horton's bowl. When I checked this evening, he hadn't touched it.

A couple of days ago Jon asked permission to give Horton a little bit of the shad. We have so much food in the house, Mom agreed, but Horton ended up not eating it.

He's gotten so thin. He seems comfortable, and he can get up and down furniture and laps. Sure, he mostly sleeps, but he always sleeps a lot.

I'd hoped when everybody left, especially Gabriel, Horton would start eating again. I know he was eating a little before they came, because I fed him when Jon was away.

When Julie was in the house, Jon was distracted, and even now he's spending most of his free time with her, either here or at Mrs. Nesbitt's. But she'll be gone in a couple of days, unless Alex changes his mind, and then Jon is going to have to face what's going on with Horton.

If he can. If any of us can.

Charlie popped in, just like a neighbor might, to invite us over for Sunday prayer service, followed by dinner.

Syl said yes right away and Matt nodded. Jon said he would if he could pray with Alex and Julie, and Charlie said of course, they were hoping Jon would join them.

That left Mom and me. I said yes, more for the dinner than the prayers. Mom thought about it and said she didn't have that many chances to be alone and whenever one came along, she grabbed it, so she'd stay home.

"You could come just for the dinner," Charlie said. "It won't be the same without you."

"I'll think about it," Mom said, which we all knew meant "no, thank you."

We're in and out of both houses all day long. Julie comes over every morning for lessons with Jon, and more often than not, Jon eats supper at Dad's. Syl goes over for Bible study. Mom sends me over with something for them, or Alex comes over with something for us, and Charlie and Mom have formed their own book club. One of them reads a mystery, then gives it to the other, and then they discuss it.

But Charlie always comes over here to see Mom. Mom never goes there. I can't decide if it's because she doesn't want to see Mrs. Nesbitt's house filled with other people or if it's Dad and Lisa she's avoiding. Maybe she thinks they want to avoid her. It can't be easy for Mom having them so close by, but she might think it's just as hard for them having her so near.

It's only been a few days since they moved out. Maybe by next week Mom will start visiting them.

The four of us walked over to Mrs. Nesbitt's this morning, splitting up once we got there. Jon went to the parlor, where Alex and Julie set up a little chapel, and Matt, Syl, and I stayed in the kitchen with everybody else.

Dad moved Mrs. Nesbitt's table back into the kitchen, and we sat around it for our prayer service. It made things feel more ordinary, and I was glad for that.

Someone would start a hymn and whoever knew it would join in. I asked for "Take My Hand, Precious Lord," since that was Grandma's favorite. There were some prayers, and Syl talked about the peace she felt when she accepted Christ as her savior. I guess that happened after the moon goddess Diana proved to be such a dud.

Charlie gave a sermon, if you could call it that. He said he'd been thinking a lot about Noah and his family lately, what it must have been like for them those 40 days and 40 nights. As far as they knew, they were the only people left on Earth. Everybody would be descended from them but only if they survived, and they had to trust in God that they would.

"I bet the rabbits weren't worried about that," Charlie said. "They just did what rabbits do. But it's our curse and our blessing to remember the past and to know there's a future."

He reached over, touched Lisa with his right hand and Syl with his left. "Our past is gone," he said. "But our future is in this house right now. Little Gabriel, sleeping peacefully in his crib. The children Syl will bear. Miranda and Julie, too. Their babies, born and unborn, are God's gift to the future, just as the ark was."

Dad squeezed Lisa's hand. Matt squeezed Syl's. I felt very much a part of something and very much alone.

Alex, Julie, and Jon came in, and Dad and Lisa served us dinner. It was crowded in the kitchen, and we couldn't all fit around the table. Dad, Matt, and Alex ate standing by the sink.

We never used to have Sunday dinner. Sunday was for track meets and skating competitions and baseball games. But even with a beef jerky main course, Sunday dinner felt special.

"I should get back to Mom," I said.

"I'll walk you home," Alex said.

It felt funny to be outside without needing a coat. It felt funny to be walking with a boy. It felt funny and awful to think in a couple of days I wouldn't see him again. He and Julie would be like all the other people who'd been part of my life and then left me.

"Have you changed your mind?" I asked him. "About Julie staying?"

"No," he said. "Did you think I would?"

I shook my head. "I'm still hoping, though," I said. "And that you'll stay, too."

"We're leaving on Tuesday," he said. "It's better for everybody. There'll be more food for you."

"Thank you for being so noble," I said. "But we'd rather be hungry with you."

Alex laughed. It surprises me every time he does.

Then he surprised me again. "You would have been my dream girl," he said. "Before. Beautiful and smart and funny and kind."

"I don't have to be," I said. "A dream, I mean. I'm here. You're here. Why leave?"

"Because it's best," he said. "Maybe not now, this minute, but for the future."

"You drive me crazy," I said. "You. Charlie. Everybody. You talk about the future like you're so sure we're going to have one."

"You have to believe in the future," Alex said. "Otherwise there's no point being alive."

"That's easy for you to say!" I cried. "You have your faith, your church. But I don't believe like that. Maybe I used to but I don't anymore."

I thought Alex would get angry at me then, but he didn't. "You don't have to believe in the church," he said. "Or even in God. Believe that people can change things."

"No," I said. "I don't know that anymore." My mind flashed back to the dead man with his dog lying beside him. "We're all helpless," I said. "There's nothing we can do. There's nothing left to trust in."

"Trust in tomorrow," Alex said. "Every day of your life, there's been a tomorrow. I promise you, there'll be a tomorrow."

"Do you trust in tomorrow?" I asked.

"I have to," he said. "For Julie's sake."

"But you don't trust in us," I said. "To look after Julie." He answered with silence.

"You don't trust in anything, either," I said. "Not really. Your God, your church, your tomorrow. You don't even trust Carlos. You're just doing what he tells you because it's easier."

"That's not true," Alex said. "You don't understand."

"I do understand," I said. "But I don't care. I'm not a dream girl. I'm a real human being with real feelings. How can I trust tomorrow? Tomorrow terrifies me. I wake up every morning scared and I go to bed every night scared, and all those tomorrows I've lived through are exactly the same. Hunger and fear and loneliness. Exactly the same as you, as everybody. Only you're worse, because when we ask you to share our hunger and our fear and our loneliness, you turn your back on us. I may be lonely and scared and hungry, but I haven't given up on loving people yet. You have. Or maybe you never loved anyone. Maybe all your life was dreams."

Alex grabbed me. I knew he would. I knew he'd kiss me, and he did, and I kissed back. Only it wasn't a dream-girl kiss. It wasn't a kiss of love or even excitement, not the way I've been kissed before.

There was so much anger in his kiss. In mine, too. We shared it, the electric volt, and when we broke away from each other, we were both shaking.

"I'm sorry," he said. "For everything." He gestured wildly, as though he was taking responsibility for the last horrible year of my life.

"It's okay," I said. "It was just a dream."

I walked the rest of the way home alone.

June 19

I was nervous someone would suggest that Alex and I go into town to get our food, but Dad and Jon ended up going instead.

Alex and Julie came over this evening to thank us for our hospitality and to say good-bye. Julie looked a wreck and Alex didn't look much better, and when they left, Jon ran to his room and hasn't come out since.

I wish Alex would go already. I wish he would never leave.

Chapter 13

June 20

The first official day of summer.

I checked the thermometer and it was close to 60. But then it started to rain, and it never stopped.

Jon spent the day sulking. I did, too. Matt and Syl spent it in their room, but I doubt they were sulking.

I don't know if Alex and Julie left. He was so determined, but the weather was awful.

I could have gone to Dad's to find out, but I didn't want Alex to know I cared. Assuming he's still there. Which he probably isn't, because he's a total idiot who would take his sister out in a hurricane if his big brother told him to.

The last living boy in America can go to hell for all I care. Except I do care, and he's probably already there.

June 21

It's still raining.

Charlie dropped over to talk mysteries with Mom. "Alex and Julie haven't left yet," he said. "Julie's developed a bit of a cough. We were wondering if you had any cough medicine around."

Mom gave Jon what little we have left, and he raced over with it. He didn't come back until after supper.

June 22

The third straight day of rain. Jon says Alex and Julie haven't left yet.

My guess is rain or snow, they'll go tomorrow. And I'll be glad. Not for Jon, who'll be heartbroken, or for Julie. Not for Alex, either, because I don't care what he feels.

I'll be glad for me. Once Alex is gone, I'll never have to think of him again. I'll throw him onto the mound of bodies and forget I ever met him.

Why not? He's already forgotten me.

June 23

It stopped raining. The ground is nothing but mud.

"I don't see how they could possibly go," Mom said to Matt and Jon and me at our rice and beans breakfast. "The convent is ninety miles from here. That's a four-day walk."

"They might be able to pick up bikes on the way," Matt said.

"They still have to find them," Mom said. "And who knows where they'll sleep. They've got to wait for things to dry out before they go."

That was all Jon needed to hear. Off he ran.

"I hope they're gone," Matt said. "The longer they stay, the harder it's going to be on Jon. And I'll be just as glad never to see Alex again."

"Why do you say that?" Mom asked.

"He's a parasite," Matt said. "He's a danger chopping wood. I'm always worried he's going to cut off one of his fingers or one of mine. I don't think he's done a day's worth of physical labor in his life. He sits and he reads and he eats our food. Which we'll run out of soon enough anyway."

"It's thanks to Alex we have food," I said. "He's the one who found it and figured out how to get it back here. He was the one who made us search the whole house." I pictured the half-eaten man and shuddered.

"It's great you found all that food," Matt said. "But it isn't going to happen again. In the meantime Alex eats what little we have. And I don't like the way he plays up to Dad."

"He doesn't play up to Dad," I said. "Dad loves him. There's a difference."

"Why does Dad love him, then?" Matt said. "It's not because of anything he does."

"I don't know," I said. "But Dad loves Syl, too, and she doesn't do anything, either."

"Miranda," Mom said, but it was too late.

"Don't you ever speak about my wife that way!" Matt shouted. "She's given up everything to be with me!"

"To get your food, you mean!" I shouted right back. "To have a place to sleep and people who wait on her hand and foot!"

We were sitting on the floor around the woodstove. Matt lunged for me.

"Matt, stop it!" Mom screamed, and I think that startled Matt into stopping. I got up and ran out of the sunroom, down the path to Mrs. Nesbitt's.

Matt's my big brother. We used to fight when we were kids. But he always knew when to stop.

This time I don't think he would have known when.

I found Alex standing outside the house, checking the sky, examining the mud. I ran straight into his arms, and before I could catch my breath, we were kissing. No rage this time. Just hunger and need.

"No," he said. At least that's what I think he said. I know I wouldn't have thought it on my own.

"Stay with us," I said. "Don't leave me."

"I have to," he said. "Julie can't stay here. We've got to go."

"But I don't want you to!" I cried like a five-year-old.

Alex kissed me and I didn't feel five anymore. I wasn't a kid having a tantrum because someone took my favorite toy. I was a woman, and this was the man I wanted, and I was losing him.

We held on to each other, not wanting the moment to end, because when it did, our life together would also end. Our kisses grew deeper, our hands explored more, we gave each other all we could in that single passing moment.

June 24

Matt's gone back to chopping wood. He insisted Jon work with him.

Mom and I cleaned the house. Charlie dropped by to invite us over for Sunday prayers and dinner.

"How's Julie doing?" Mom asked.

"She's a little better," Charlie said. "The cough medicine seems to have helped. Hal's convinced Alex to stay until Tuesday. Let's hope the weather's better this week."

"I think I'll see how she's doing," I said. "Mom, is there anything I can bring?"

"I don't think so," Mom said. "I gave them the last of our cough medicine."

"Well, I'll check and see, anyway," I said. I didn't even sound convincing to myself.

When I got there, Lisa was playing with Gabriel. Of course once he saw me, he began crying.

"He's allergic to me," I said, and Lisa laughed.

"He's ready for his nap," she said. "Julie's resting now. Alex is in the parlor, though, if you want to see him."

"I guess so," I said, and walked through the house as casually as I could. All I wanted to do was fling myself into his arms. Alex must have felt the same way because he gestured for me to be quiet. We slipped out the front door and ran far from the house.

"This is wrong," he said as we embraced. "We have to stop."

"Stopping is wrong," I said, kissing him to prove my point.

He pulled away. "Miranda, listen to me," he said. "We can't do this. I'm leaving in two days. I'll never see you again. You have to believe that."

It's funny. That's all I've heard for weeks now, how Alex and Julie will be leaving. Maybe because they talk and talk and talk about it but never actually go, I've stopped believing it.

"What if Julie isn't ready?" I asked. "What if she's still sick next week?"

"She can't be," Alex said. "I have to get her to the sisters while I can. She has to be with people who'll protect her."

"You'll protect her," I said. "We'll protect her. And don't use Carlos as an excuse anymore. He's thousands of miles away. You're here. I'm here. Explain why getting Julie to the convent is more important than you and me. Because I try to understand, Alex. I hear the words, but I don't get the meaning."

Alex kissed me, and when he held on to me, I felt how reluctant he was to open up, how scared.

"It's all right," I said. "Just tell me."

He looked straight at me, and once again I could see all the suffering in his eyes. "New York was very bad," he said. "Every day you'd think, Well this is as bad as it can get, and then it got worse. I saw things, I did things, things I never want you to know."

"You could tell me anything," I said, but he interrupted me.

"I love you for thinking that, but you're wrong," he said. "You can't imagine what things were like. Carlos couldn't understand. He got to Texas in the very beginning, and the Marines have fed him, sheltered him, protected him."

"Has Julie seen those things?" I asked.

He nodded.

"She survived," I said. "I could, too. Alex, don't feel like you have to protect me. That's not what I want."

"I can't protect you," he said. "I can't protect anyone. I can't even do what Carlos tells me and get Julie to the convent. The rain stops me. You stop me."

I kissed him, hoping the gift of my love could ease his pain. But he broke away.

"I won't let Julie suffer," he said. "I tried to tell Carlos but I couldn't. There is too much past history between us."

"Julie doesn't have to suffer," I said. "Not if she stays with us."

He shook his head. "You have no control," he said. "None of us do. Not over what might happen. I have only one way left to protect Julie. Everything else I've tried has failed."

"What?" I asked, figuring he'd say faith or prayers or the church.

Alex took a deep breath. "Pills," he said. "Sleeping pills. Six of them. I got them in New York. I keep them for her."

"So she can sleep?" I asked.

"So she won't ever wake up," Alex said.

"Six pills wouldn't be enough," I said, like if I told him that, he would laugh at how silly he was, and nothing would matter except us.

"Two would be enough," he said instead. "Enough to make sure she'd sleep through what I'd do."

"But why?" I asked. "Why would you do something like that?"

"There could come a time when life is worse than death for Julie," Alex said. "I'll know it when it does. I pray I'll know it."

"But killing's a crime," I said.

"Nothing's a crime anymore," he said. "There are no cops, no jails. It's a sin, and I'll be damned for it. But I'll deserve damnation. I deserve it now."

"You don't," I said. "You love Julie. You love me. How can you be damned for loving?"

"Love isn't enough," he said.

"It has to be," I said, holding his shaking body in my arms. "Love's what I believe in, Alex. Love is what protects us."

June 25

Last night I had a dream that the doorbell rang, and when I opened it, there was Alex. It was summer, and he was holding a bouquet of daisies.

"Julie's a nun," he said. "So's Carlos. Marry me, Miranda."

I'm not going to write what happened next in my dream, in case anyone ever sees this. Let's just say it was the best dream I ever had.

When I woke up, I thought maybe things could happen that way. Not with Julie and Carlos becoming nuns. But maybe if Alex was sure Julie was safe, he'd come back to me. I know he loves me. That has to count for something.

Alex has convinced me it's better for Julie to be at the convent. I hate the thought of his having her life in his hands. Not that he'd ever do anything to Julie. But he shouldn't have to worry about it. He's taken care of Julie for over a year now. He'd take care of her forever, except Carlos told him not to.

Maybe it's wrong of me to dream that Alex and I can stay together if Julie's at the convent. Maybe it's wrong of me to want that when I know Julie doesn't want to go.

But Carlos is the one who made the decision, and Carlos is right that Julie should be someplace safe, where he and Alex will always be able to find her. And Julie can take care of herself. She'll stay at the convent for as long as she has to, and then she'll do what she wants. Assuming she can. Assuming any of us can.

If he doesn't have to worry about Julie, I know Alex will stay with me. We can't be together as long as Julie is here. But when she's at the convent, Alex will be free to stay with me forever.

I want Alex. I want love. I know that's what Alex wants also.

Jon and Syl went over to Dad's this morning. Mom told Jon if it was all right with Alex, he and Julie could make the food run.

I feel strange around Syl since my fight with Matt. I don't think he told her what I said but I can't be sure. I was glad when she decided to visit Lisa for Bible study.

I planned on going over to see Alex one last time, but before I could figure out an excuse, Dad, Alex, and Matt showed up. Matt had been chopping wood, so I knew this was important.

For a moment I thought Dad would tell us he'd forbidden Alex to leave, and Alex would come to his senses and agree.

"I wanted to talk with you," Dad said, meaning Mom and Matt, I guess, but he didn't tell me to leave, so I didn't. "Without anyone else around."

"We're leaving tomorrow," Alex said. "Julie's cough is gone. Thank you for the cough medicine, Mrs. Evans. It made a big difference."

"I'm glad," Mom said. "I'm glad Julie's well again."

"You know this scheme of Alex's," Dad said. "And you know I don't approve. Lisa's distraught, and Jon isn't much better."

"I know how upset Jon is," Mom said, "but he'll get over it in time."

"He'll have to," Alex said. "We've waited too long as it is."

"The convent is ninety miles away," Dad said.

"We've walked farther," Alex said. "And in worse weather."

"That may be," Dad said. "But in this case it isn't necessary. There's the van in the garage. With two five-gallon gas cans."

"Are you crazy?" Matt asked. "We're supposed to give away the van? That's our way out of here, Dad. We don't hand that over to strangers."

"Alex found the van," I said. "And the gas."

"You were with him," Matt said. "He couldn't have found them without you. They're as much ours as his, and our need is greater."

"You should be ashamed of yourself, Matt," Dad said. "Julie's just a child."

"So is Jon," Matt said. "That didn't stop you from leaving."

"Stop it," Mom said. "Both of you. Now."

Alex has never heard that tone from Mom. It's probably been years since Dad has.

"Alex, are you absolutely determined that you and Julie are going tomorrow?" Mom asked. "You know how much we've come to care about you. In spite of that you're going?"

"Yes, Mrs. Evans," Alex said. "First thing tomorrow morning."

"After Julie is settled in, what will you do?" Mom asked.

"There's a Franciscan monastery in Ohio," Alex said, and Matt snickered.

"Matthew, stop that right now," Mom said.

"Mom," Matt said. "I'm not a child anymore."

"Then stop acting like one," Mom said, turning away from him. "So your plan is to go northeast for ninety miles and then make your way across Pennsylvania to get to Ohio. That's hundreds of miles."

"We made it from Texas here," Alex replied. "I can make it from New York to Ohio."

"It won't be the same," Dad said. "The farther north, the fewer people."

"It's summer," Alex said. "It's warmer. I'll do it."

"Fine," Mom said. "It's your choice and we're not your parents. Julie's the one I'm concerned about. Why not drive to the convent and return the van on your way to Ohio?"

"What makes you think he'll bring it back?" Matt said.

"He'll bring it back," I cried. "I know he will."

Everyone stared at me.

"I trust him," I said, my voice shaking. "We can trust him."

"Alex, will you give us your solemn word that you'll bring the van back once you're certain Julie's all right?" Mom asked.

"I'm not accepting his solemn word," Matt said. "It's not good enough. These are our lives we're talking about. If Dad won't look after Miranda and Jon, then I will."

"I'll take Alex and Julie," Dad said. "I'll drive them to the convent and then Alex and I can drive back."

"You'll use up all the gas," Matt said. "The van's got to be a gas guzzler."

"Couldn't Alex take one of the cars instead?" I asked. "Matt's or Mrs. Nesbitt's? They'd get better mileage, and we'd have the van if we need it."

"That's a great idea, Miranda," Dad said. "Five gallons in a car will get us farther than ten gallons in the van. We'll use one of the containers and leave the other one here for an emergency."

"That seems fair to me," I said, glaring at Matt. "Alex can use his half of the gas and we'll keep my half here."

"How do we know the cars are still working?" Mom asked.

"You didn't keep them tuned up?" Dad asked. "All these months and you didn't run the engines?"

"It was stupid of me," Mom said. She looked stricken. "Hal, I didn't think. I'm sorry."

"I thought I could count on you," he said to Matt.

"Well, I thought I could count on you," Matt replied. "I guess we were both wrong."

I hated this. I hated every moment of it. These are the people I love most in the world and the ones I depend on the most. "Maybe the cars still run," I said. "We won't know until we try. And if they don't, then Alex should take the van. He can have my half of the gas. Maybe Dad'll find some more gas on the drive back."

"If the van is all you have, Julie and I can't take it," Alex said. "We'll go by foot. We'll find bikes along the way, maybe another car. We can manage."

"No," Mom said. "The air is awful, and Julie shouldn't be out in it any longer than necessary. Hal, if you drive Julie and Alex, when do you think you'll get back? Tomorrow night?"

"Maybe," Dad said. "Or Wednesday afternoon. That way we could make sure Julie's settled in. And there's no way of knowing what the roads are like."

"Lisa and Gabriel can stay over here," Mom said. "If they'll feel more comfortable."

"No, they'll be fine," Dad said. "Charlie will look after them. Maybe Jon could spend the night."

"Then it's settled," Mom said. "And I don't want to hear another word out of any of you." She glared equal time at Alex and Matt.

"Miranda, would you like to come along?" Dad asked. "I'd love your company, and I'm sure Alex and Julie would, too."

"Yes," I said before anyone had a chance to say no for me.

"Is that a good idea?" Mom asked. "Ninety miles. That seems so far away."

"Please, Mom," I said. "I never go anywhere. You let Matt and Jon go all by themselves to the river. I'll be in the van with Dad."

Mom hesitated. "Alex, would you mind?" she asked.

"No ma'am," he said. "I think it would be easier on Julie if Miranda was with us. On Hal, too."

"He's right," Dad said. "It would make losing Julie hurt a little bit less."

"You'll be back by Wednesday?" Mom said. "You and Miranda?"

"I don't see why not," Dad said. "Maybe even tomorrow night."

Matt shook his head. "It's a bad idea," he said.

"I'm not sure it's a good one," Mom said. "But all right. Miranda can go."

I got up and hugged her and then I hugged Dad. As I broke away from him, my hand touched Alex's.

Alex and I will be together, I thought. We'll see that Julie is safe together, and then he'll know he belongs with me.

Chapter 14

When I got to Dad's this morning, I found Lisa in a state of hysterics.

"How can you take her from me?" she was screaming at Alex. "Hal, don't let him. I'll hate you both if you take her away."

Gabriel, who doesn't need much excuse to get going, was screaming almost as loudly.

"I don't want to go," Julie said. "Alex, don't make me go."

Alex yelled something in Spanish at her, which shut her up. Charlie picked up Gabriel and soothed him. Dad held Lisa, stroking her back until she calmed down.

"She'll only be ninety miles away," Dad said, which used to mean "We can visit on weekends" but now means "That's not quite the end of the earth."

"She's the only person who understands," Lisa said. "The rest of you just pretend to. Julie knows what I've gone through not knowing what happened to my parents, my sisters."

"I'm sorry, Lisa," Alex said. "But I have to take her. Hal, can we go now?"

"We'd better," Dad said. "Lisa, darling, I'll be back tonight. Tomorrow at the latest." He kissed her and Gabriel, hugged Charlie, and half pushed Julie out of the house. Alex did the other half of the pushing.

I thought Julie might cry, but she was silent, the way Alex can be. I had mixed feelings. I knew I'd miss Julie, and I felt bad for Jon and Lisa. But I was excited at the thought of leaving Howell for the first time in over a year. And I was so sure that once Julie was in the convent, Alex would agree to stay with me.

Julie and Alex had returned our clothes to us yesterday and had all their belongings in their backpacks. We threw our sleeping bags into the back of the old van. Mom's van and Matt's car and Mrs. Nesbitt's car hadn't started when Dad tried them last night, and Matt was so angry at himself that he picked a fight with Syl. They stayed up half the night yelling at each other.

Jon was mad, too. He'd gone over to Dad's last night to say good-bye, but Mom refused to let him go again this morning. So he was curled up in a corner of the dining room, trying not to cry.

It seemed like an excellent time to get away from home.

Dad did the driving, and I sat next to him. If you didn't know better, you'd think we were a family, maybe a divorced dad bringing his kids back to their mom after a long weekend. Of course we were a bilingual family, since the only conversation I could hear between Alex and Julie was whispered in Spanish.

Even on the highway Dad stuck to 30 miles an hour. The engine sputtered, and at one point it overheated, and Dad stopped driving until it cooled down. I didn't mind. Everything was gloomy and gray and there were no signs of life anywhere, but it was still thrilling to be away, and there was no hurry to get back home. Alex and I had all the time in the world to be together.

I realized the second time Dad stopped to let the car cool down that I might never get this far from home again. Mom wasn't going to leave, with food still coming to us and electricity practically every day and with as much wood as we'd ever need to stay warm. Syl might want to go (that seemed to be one of the things she and Matt fought about last night), but Matt won't leave Mom or the rest of us behind. I guess if Dad and Lisa leave, Jon might go with them. But why would Lisa go anywhere, when traveling's dangerous for the baby.

So this trip was it for me, summer camp and college and honeymoon all rolled into one. The fact that it was going to end at a convent didn't dampen my excitement. It's not like I've ever been to a convent before.

"How do you know about this place?" I asked after I'd gotten sufficiently bored trying to figure out what Alex and Julie were going on about. "From the Fresh Air Fund?"

"No," Alex said. "Our priest told me about it a year ago. They were taking girls in, but Julie was too young then."

Julie muttered something in Spanish. Alex muttered back.

"If your priest approved of it, it must be a good place," Dad said.

"Yes," Alex said. "That's why Carlos thought it would be good for Julie."

"There'll be girls your age there, Julie," Dad said. "That will be nice for you, having friends again."

"Jon was my friend," Julie said, which set Alex off on a Spanish torrent.

Dad ignored him. "Jon's going to miss you," he said. "We all will."

"It's for the best," Alex said. "Julie's going to a safe place. God will look after her there."

"That's a comfort, I'm sure," Dad said, slamming on the brakes. "We'd better clear those branches off the road," he said. "I can't risk driving over them."

"I'll do it," I said. Alex joined me. Dad had done a good job driving over and around potholes, but the roads were in awful condition, littered with branches and other garbage. Mostly it wasn't a problem, but occasionally we had to stop and clear things out of the way.

"I hadn't realized you've known about the convent that long," I said. It made me feel better to learn that Julie would have been at the convent for a year if she'd been old enough to go last summer.

"It's a good place," he said. "The sisters will look after her. They'll learn to love her."

"We have," I said.

Alex nodded. "You've been very good to her," he said. "Your family's been very kind to both of us." He grabbed the biggest branch and dragged it to the side of the road while I carried some smaller ones. I looked through the front window of the van and could see Dad had turned around to talk to Julie.

"Things will be all right," I said softly. "For Julie. For us."

"I would love you forever if I could," he said.

"You can," I said, wanting desperately to hold him. But all I could do was brush my hand quickly against his. For a second he clutched my hand in his.

We got back in the car, and Dad resumed his slow drive through New York. Alex and Julie had nothing more to say to each other in any language, and Dad gave up trying to make small talk. I could see he was worried about the van, but he didn't say anything about it.

We made one pit stop, which was pretty literally that. We'd brought some food with us, but we were saving it for supper. Nothing was open, none of the strip malls we passed or the occasional motel or gas station. I thought about how Matt had met Syl at a motel and wondered if any of the ones on the side of the road had people camping out in them, but there were no signs of life.

We drove ninety miles without seeing another car, and the scariest thing was that seemed normal.

"It's hard to believe there are still people out there," I said. "Is everyone living in evac centers and cities?"

"It seems that way, doesn't it," Dad said. "But there were plenty of people on the road. There were days we didn't run into anybody else, but for the most part you'd see someone new every day."

"Syl told me bands of people came together and split apart," I said. "I guess your band stayed together, all of you and Charlie."

"Charlie was the glue," Dad said. "He never let us give up."

"It's amazing," I said. "It really is. You traveled thousands of miles, and Dad, you're back with us, and now Julie's going to this convent Alex has known about for a year. It really is amazing."

"Christ has blessed us," Alex said.

"Yes, He has," Dad said.

Well, that was a conversation stopper.

We made two more stops, one to cool down the engine and one to clear off the road, and then we got to the town.

Like everything else, it was completely deserted. It had been a charming town once, you could tell. There were antique stores and bakeries with French names and tea shoppes. But now it was a ghost town like Howell, only worse, because I know there are people in Howell.

"The convent is on Whitlock Lane," Alex said. "Off Albany Post Road."

"We should be able to find it, then," Dad said. "Albany Post Road is generally the biggest street in these towns, like Main Street. We'll see where it takes us."

It took us through neighborhoods with empty streets. But amazingly, or maybe miraculously, we saw the road sign for Notburga Farms.

"That's it," Alex said. "That's its name."

Dad made a left, and we drove for a couple of miles on Whitlock Lane. The road was in bad shape, and we had to stop a couple of times to move debris. It was a relief when we saw the Notburga Farms sign.

We looked out at a field. You could imagine how beautiful it must have been a year ago, a large green expanse surrounded by an apple orchard. But now the ground was gray and the trees had only a few sickly leaves.

It could have been anywhere. It could have been Howell.

I got out and opened the gate. Dad followed the driveway to the convent. It was an old farmhouse, with outbuildings, barns, and what looked to be a chapel.

"I don't think there's anyone here," Dad said.

"No," Alex said. "There must be. I asked about it at the archdiocese in Louisville. It was listed as open."

"Alex, that was months ago," Dad said. "Anything could have happened."

"We're going in," Alex said. "I won't believe the sisters deserted this place until I see it for myself. Come on, Julie."

We all got out of the van. Alex led the way, knocking boldly on the farmhouse door.

"Who is it?" a querulous voice asked. "Sister Grace, is that you?"

"No," Alex said. "Please open the door. I've brought my sister for you to take care of."

We could hear footsteps, and then an elderly woman nervously unlocked the door. "Did Sister Grace send you?" she asked.

"No," Alex said. "Father Franco in New York did. May I speak with you privately, Sister?"

"I'm all alone," the nun said. "Sister Grace told Sister Anne and Sister Monica to take the girls back to New York City and to stay there. That was October, I think. A few weeks ago Sister Grace said she'd better get help for us so she and Sister Marie left, and then it was only Sister Helen and me. Sister Helen passed away three days ago. Or maybe it was four. It's so hard to keep track of time. I'm all alone now. Do you know where Sister Grace is?"

"No, Sister," Alex said. "But we brought food. We can give you our food."

"That would be very kind of you," the nun said. "Please come in."

"We haven't been introduced," Dad said. "My name is Hal Evans, and this is my daughter, Miranda, and our friends Alex and Julie Morales."

"I'm Sister Paulina," she said. "I was in charge of the dairy, but we slaughtered the cows months ago. There was no feed for them. The meat kept us alive until Easter."

I couldn't bear it. "I'll get the food," I said, glad for any excuse to get away from her and the house. It reeked of death, and I realized that Sister Helen must still be there, rotting away.

It was awful. I remembered finding Mrs. Nesbitt lying on her bed the morning she died. I left her there, went through her house searching for food, for anything we could use, before going home to tell Matt and Jon and Mom that she had died.

At the time it seemed so right to do that. Now I asked myself what kind of monster was I, that I could carefully examine every inch of a house knowing that a beloved friend was lying dead while I looked.

I took the food from the van and slowly carried it to the farmhouse. The smell must have been too much for everybody, because they were all sitting on the porch, looking out onto the gray deserted field.

"It's so nice to have company," Sister Paulina was saying as I approached. "I don't know when Grace and Marie will be back, though. It's been so long. You'd think if they'd found help, they would have returned by now."

"Here," I said, thrusting the bag of food at her. "It's all the food we brought with us."

"This is so kind," Sister Paulina said. "Sister Helen would have been so glad. She said she wasn't hungry, but I could see that she was. In her eyes, you know. Even at the end her eyes never lost that look."

"Maybe you should come with us, Sister Paulina," Dad said. "Back to our home in Pennsylvania."

"That's very thoughtful of you," Sister Paulina said. "But Grace left me in charge while she's gone. I couldn't possibly leave."

"Sister Grace might never return," Dad said.

"Oh, she will," Sister Paulina said. "It's only been a few weeks, and nowadays everything takes so long. I worry that Marie has taken sick. There's been so much illness. We did what we could for the people in town, but so many died. I suppose they've all left by now, the ones who survived. It used to be people would bring us food and firewood, but no one's come for a very long time. We had hoped at Easter we'd be remembered, but it was just the four of us."

"Please," Dad said. "You'll die here if you stay alone."

"I'll die anyway," Sister Paulina said. "I made my peace with that a long time ago." She smiled, but it wasn't a crazy-lady smile. It was the smile of someone who wasn't afraid of death.

"We'll stay with you," Alex said. "Julie and I. Until Sister Grace gets back."

"Alex," Dad said.

"No, Hal," Alex said. "It's the right thing for us to do."

"It's sweet of you to offer," Sister Paulina said. "But Sister Grace didn't give me permission to open the convent to others, so I'm afraid I'll have to say no."

"Is there anything we can do for you while we're here?" Dad asked.

"Why yes," Sister Paulina said. "Helen's been lying in her bed all these days. She looks so peaceful, but I think it would be for the best if she were buried. Don't you agree? Dust to dust."

"We can do that," Dad said. "Tell us where we can find shovels."

Sister Paulina rose and pointed to one of the outbuildings. "That's the toolshed," she said. "Helen was in charge of the vegetable garden. Oh, she had a green thumb. Tomatoes so sweet you could eat them for dessert. Zucchini and carrots and corn. All summer long we'd eat from her garden, and then we'd can what we didn't eat. It was a wonderful life." She looked out at the apple trees. "No crop this year," she said. "If God is merciful, next year the bounty will return."

"God is merciful," Dad said. "I believe in His mercy."

"I used to," Sister Paulina said. "I suppose I will again someday. After all, you people have brought me food. And you're going to help with Helen."

Dad nodded. "It's going to take a while," he said. "We'd better get started. Come on, Alex."

"Could we walk around?" Julie asked. "I've heard so much about the farm, I'd like to see it."

"Certainly, dear," Sister Paulina said. "You'll forgive me if I don't join you? My arthritis is kicking up today. I think it will rain tomorrow."

"Want to come?" Julie asked me, and I was more than willing. We never walked so far we couldn't see the farmhouse, but we were too far away to hear any conversation or to be overheard.

"There's no reason why you and Alex can't stay with us now," I said.

Julie shook her head. "Alex'll find another convent to take me," she said. "Between here and Ohio. The archdiocese in Pittsburgh will know where there's one. Then he'll go to the monastery."

"He doesn't have to," I said. "Carlos won't know any better."

"It's not just Carlos," Julie said. "Alex wants to go to the monastery."

What Alex wanted was me. But there was no way Julie could know that, or at least know the depth of his feelings.

"Maybe he'll change his mind," I said. "You said he didn't always want to be a monk."

"That was before," Julie said. "Alex explained it to me when we were in Kentucky. He said God had entrusted me to him and that once he knew I was safe, he would dedicate his life to Christ in gratitude."

"People change their minds," I said.

"Not Alex," Julie said. "Even when he's wrong, he doesn't change his mind."

I realized then that I knew Alex better than she did. But Julie would never believe me if I said that, any more than I'd believe Syl if she said it about Matt.

"Alex loves you," I said. "He wants what's best for you. So does Carlos. You're lucky to have them."

Julie shook her head. "They may love me, but they don't want me," she said. "Neither of them wants me. But it doesn't matter. The Holy Mother will look after me until I can look after myself."

"We'll look after you," I said. "Mom and Dad and Lisa and Charlie. Jon. You're part of our family now. You and Alex both are."

"We have no family," she said. "Not anymore. Come on. We should go back."

I let her lead me to the farmhouse. When we got there, Sister Paulina, Alex, and Dad were kneeling in prayer. Julie joined them. I felt uncomfortable standing and watching, but I knew I'd feel even more uncomfortable joining them.

Then Alex and Dad went upstairs, and a few minutes later they brought down Sister Helen. They'd wrapped her in a blanket, but it didn't matter. It was obviously difficult for them to carry her, and Julie, without hesitating, walked over to help. I had no choice but to do the same.

We carried her outside, Sister Paulina by our side. Dad and Alex lowered the body gently into the hole they'd dug. Alex, Julie, and the Sister recited some prayers, and then Dad and Alex filled the hole with dirt.

We didn't stay much after that. It was still early, but the sky was getting dark. Sister Paulina kissed all of us good-bye and thanked us, and said she'd tell Sister Grace about our visit when she got back. Which we all knew she never would.

We were back on the road for less than two hours when the van stopped. We could feel it die.

Dad got out, lifted the hood, and acted like he knew what the matter was. Alex joined him. They looked manly and stupid and only got back in when rain began to fall.

"We'll sleep in the van," Dad said. "We'll start for home in the morning."

"How far are we?" Julie asked.

"About forty miles, I'd say," Dad replied.

"That's two days walking," Alex said. "Three if the weather stays bad."

"We can do it," Dad said. "We'll be home by Thursday."

None of us said anything, but we all knew that's two days of hard walking on no food. The longer we go without eating, the harder the walking will be.

So that's where we are. The rain is pelting against the roof of the van. Dad's sitting behind the wheel, staring out the front window, thinking about Lisa probably, and Mom, and how upset they're going to be. Alex and Julie are in the back, whispering furiously in Spanish. I'd brought my diary and a flashlight pen on a just-in-case basis, so I'm in the passenger seat, writing all this down. The more I concentrate on what happened, the less I have to worry about what's going to happen.

June 28

We're camping out in a gas station convenience store. It's crowded with the four of us, there's no food (we looked everywhere), the roof leaks, and the windows have all been smashed in. But the toilet works, so I guess we're in paradise.

We stopped before it got dark because Julie was coughing. I don't know how much farther I could have gone anyway.

Dad says we made good progress today, and he thinks we're about twenty miles from home. We should be home by tomorrow night.

"I want to tell you how proud I am of you," he said. "A year ago I had three children. Now I have seven. The world is a mess, and you have every right to be angry and scared, but things will get better. You'll make it better."

"We'll do our best," Alex said.

Dad smiled. "Life's sloppy," he said. "You think you know how tomorrow is going to be, you've made your plans, everything is set in place, and then the unimaginable happens. Life catches you by surprise. It always does. But there's good mixed in with the bad. It's there. You just have to recognize it."

My feet are blistered from all the unaccustomed walking. My body is shaking from cold and hunger and exhaustion. I'm frightened I'll never see home again and almost more frightened that once I get there, I'll never leave.

I know Dad's right that there's good mixed in with the bad. But I don't know that I'll ever have the wisdom to recognize it.

June 29

We're still in New York, but we're close to the border. We're spending the night in an empty house. There are beds and pillows and blankets.

Dad and Alex went out looking for bikes or a car with some gas. I fantasized they'd find some food. But when they came back, they had nothing.

It was foggy most of the morning, and with the ash, it was like breathing mud. We had to take break after break because we were coughing too hard to move on.

I had a horrible nightmare last night, and I couldn't shake it from my mind today.

I dreamed we were in the convenience store, Dad and Julie and me zipped in our sleeping bags. Only Alex was up. First he went to Julie and forced her to swallow two pills. Then he forced Dad to swallow two.

When he got to me, I tried to free my arms from the sleeping bag, but I was trapped. I couldn't move my body. I felt helpless as Alex knelt beside me. He gently lifted my head, resting it in the crook of his arm. Almost in spite of myself, I felt an overwhelming hunger for him, and when he bent over and kissed me, I welcomed his lips, his mouth, the proof of his love, until I tasted the sleeping pills on his tongue.

I woke up shaking. There was enough light coming through the broken windows that I could see everyone's faces. Even in sleep Alex looked troubled.

I love Alex. I love loving Alex. I love his touch and I love remembering his touch. For so long I thought I would never have someone to love, and now I do. Every day I'm with him is a day I never believed possible.

Tonight Alex is sleeping in the room next to mine. I want him so much. I want the wall between us to dissolve, for us to be alone, to be together, to be one.

Then my doubts would be gone. My nightmares would be gone.

All there would be is Alex and me.

Two bodies. One heart.

June 30

We're home.

Horton is dead.

I'm crying too hard to write.

July

Chapter 15

July 1

I slept most of today.

Jon still refuses to come home.

Matt went to Dad's, but Jon wouldn't talk to him. Dad told Matt that Jon's angry at him for bringing Syl home. Syl's in their bedroom, so she didn't hear, but Matt whispered everything to Mom anyway. Maybe he didn't want me to hear either, but I did.

Syl tried to talk to me, to explain why she did it, but Mom said I was too tired to talk about anything and Syl's explanations would have to wait.

I know I'm going to have to talk to her. We live under the same roof, and I can't move in with Dad the way Jon has. It wouldn't be fair to Mom or to everyone there. Alex has to figure out what he and Julie are going to do, and the way she's been coughing, they can't go anytime soon. That would make seven of us there, not counting Gabriel, and three here, and that's not a good idea.

But I don't want to talk to Syl. I don't want to look at her.

I'm going to start crying again. I'm going to my closet to cry there.

Alex came over. I haven't seen him since we got home two days ago. He looked haggard.

"Mrs. Evans, you have to talk to Jon," he said. "You have to convince him to come home. It's not good for Julie having Jon there all the time."

"I'm sorry," Mom said. "When Jon's ready to accept what Syl did, he'll come back."

"Could you talk with him?" Alex asked me.

I wasn't sure what I'd say to Jon. I couldn't ask him to accept Syl's decision to let Horton go so he could die peacefully in the woods. I can't accept it, and it doesn't help that I was angry at Matt before we left for the convent and I'm even angrier now.

But Mom won't go over, which I refuse to think about because it scares me when I do, and Jon won't talk to Matt, and Dad has Lisa and Gabriel and fears of his own to deal with. And Alex looked awful.

"I'll talk with him," I said. "But I'm not going to change his mind."

"Just calm him down," Alex said.

"I'll try," I said. "But don't get your hopes up."

Jon didn't even know what Syl had done until Thursday. Mom sent Jon to stay with Lisa Tuesday night, and Syl let Horton out on Wednesday morning. Matt says that was to protect Jon, so he wouldn't be there when Horton died, but even if that's true, it wasn't Syl's decision to make. Mom was so worried about us, she didn't realize Horton was gone until Thursday.

Syl told her and Matt what she'd done, and Matt went over and told Jon. The two of them looked for hours before they found his body. Matt says he was maybe a hundred feet from the house. They just didn't know where to look.

I'm not going to cry.

Matt went back to the house and got a towel and Horton's favorite catnip mouse. He wrapped Horton up, and he and Jon buried him in Mom's old flower garden. That was Thursday afternoon, and no one knew where we were or if we were okay.

And I didn't know about Horton.

I hate Syl. I hate her doing this to Horton and to Jon and to Mom. It tears me up inside to think of Horton trying to get home but too weak to make it those last hundred feet. Or maybe that was as far as he ever got.

I knew he was dying. I think Jon knew it, too. But Horton should have been allowed to die in his own home. It was more his home than Syl's.

Charlie must have seen us as we were walking over, because he ran to join us. "I wanted to tell you how sorry I am," he said to me. "About Horton. He was..." and he paused. "He was an excellent cat."

"Thank you," I said. "He really was."

Charlie patted me on the arm and then went back to Matt.

Alex turned to me. "I'm sorry," he said, "about your cat. I never had a pet, so I don't know how you feel, but I can see how upset Jon is."

"Horton was a member of our family," I said. "It's like losing a member of your family."

Alex is like Syl, like Charlie. They don't talk about their pasts, their families. I know he has an older brother and a younger sister, but he's never told me what happened to his parents. And I don't want to think about what he's been through to make him so certain death could be preferable to life.

I have scars. No one alive today doesn't. But Alex's scars have to be much deeper than mine.

"I'm sorry," I said. "It's different. But it still hurts so much."

Alex nodded. "I wish you hadn't come on the trip," he said. "You could have been home, maybe done something."

"Horton was dying," I said. "It was a matter of time. I don't like how he died. I don't think I'll ever forgive Syl. But it was good for me to go, to see what things are really like. I needed to know."

"I thanked Christ you were with us," Alex said. "I thanked Him for every hour, every minute, with you."

"Do you mean that?" I asked.

"I'm sorry, Miranda," he said. "I'm not good at loving people. I know you're supposed to want what's best for them, but all I want is you."

"I'm here," I said, reaching out for his hand to touch. "I'm not going anywhere."

"But I am," he said. "I've got to find a place for Julie."

"Her place is here," I said. "Your place is here."

"We live on charity here," Alex said. "Your family's charity. The town's charity. Charity doesn't last."

"There's a difference between charity and love," I said. "What we're offering is love. Love lasts forever."

"It only lasts if there's something given in return," Alex said. "I helped find food, the van. I gave your family things they needed. But now all I do is take. That wasn't what I was taught, to take and not give. We have to go, Miranda. As soon as Julie's ready, we'll leave."

"Just think about it," I said.

"It's all I ever think about," he said. "Now come. Get Jon. It's not good for Julie having him here."

I followed him into the house. Gabriel was crying, and Lisa was trying to soothe him. "Julie and Jon are in the parlor," she said. "It's okay. Hal's with them."

I felt like an idiot. It took me until then to realize why Alex was so determined to separate Jon and Julie. Jon's almost fifteen; Julie's almost fourteen. They're not just talking about baseball.

But when we walked into the parlor, they weren't talking about anything. Jon and Julie were reading textbooks, and Dad was looking straight at them.

I haven't seen Jon since I got home. I didn't know what to say to him. All I knew was I couldn't cry and I couldn't tell him how angry I was at Syl.

"Hi, Julie," I said after I gave Dad a hello kiss. "How are you feeling?"

"I'm okay," she said. "I think I had a cold, but I've been okay since we got back."

"She's been coughing a little," Dad said. "But she's feeling better."

"Good," I said. "Hi, Jon."

Jon looked up at me. "I'm not going home," he said. "I don't care what you say."

"I haven't said anything," I pointed out.

"It doesn't matter," he said. "I'm not going home. Not while she's there."

"Her name is Syl," Dad said. "And you're going to have to forgive her sometime."

"I'm never going to forgive her," Jon said. "You can't make me."

"Syl let Horton die," Julie said, like this was going to be news to me. "Jon hates her for that."

"Julie, shut up," Alex said. "This isn't our business."

"Don't talk to her that way!" Jon screamed.

"Jon," Dad said. Gabriel howled in the background.

"No!" Jon yelled. "I hate all of you. Julie and I are going away. We're going to a safe town. We'll never see any of you again."

"You're not going anywhere, Jon," Dad said. "You're too young to travel on your own, and Alex won't let Julie go. There's no safe town in your future. You need connections to get passes. You can't buy them like movie tickets."

"We won't have to buy them," Jon said. "Alex has some. Julie told me. He's not using them, so we will."

I had no idea what Jon was talking about, but it was obvious Alex did. "You told him?" he said to Julie, sounding like he couldn't possibly believe she had. But then he must have believed it because he started shouting at her in Spanish, and she yelled right back.

"Stop it!" Dad said. "All of you. Right now!"

It was like a game of frozen statues. None of us moved.

I've never seen Dad so angry. "You have passes for a safe town?" he asked Alex. "What are you planning to trade them for? A truck ride to Ohio while your sister coughs to death?"

Alex looked like Dad had punched him. Then he raced out of the room, out of the house. Julie jumped up and ran after him.

"Go home, Jon," Dad said. "Go home with Miranda."

"I won't," Jon said.

"Stop acting like a child," Dad said. "I won't have it anymore."

"Please," I said to Jon. "I need you. I hate it there without you."

There was a moment when I didn't know what he would do. Jon's been so strong the past year. He's grown up so much. But there's a part of him that's still a kid.

Jon nodded. He didn't say anything more, but when we went outside, he ran to Julie. She took his hand, and after a moment's hesitation they started toward our house.

Alex watched as they walked away. He didn't move as I approached him.

"What's all this about?" I asked. "You have passes to a safe town? Does that mean you and Julie could be living in one?"

"It doesn't concern you," he said.

"If it concerns you, it concerns me," I said. "Honestly, Alex. What do I have to do to prove that to you?"

"I'm sorry," he said. He reached out and held me tightly. When our lips met, I felt like I knew everything about him. But of course there's so much I don't know.

"The safe town," I said, breaking away from him. "The passes."

"I have three passes," Alex said. "They're for family members—wives, husbands, young children. I'm past the cutoff age."

"But Julie isn't," I said. "Did Carlos know about the passes? When he decided she should go to the convent?"

"I told him everything," Alex replied. "I hoped he'd know where a safe town was. They keep them guarded. Carlos tried to find out where one was but he couldn't, so he told me to take Julie to the convent instead. Julie didn't want to go and I took her side. But Carlos insisted. Julie had to be someplace where she'd be protected, someplace where he and I could find her."

"You still have the passes?" I asked. "You held on to them all this time?"

"I kept them in reserve," he said. "I would have bartered them for Julie if I'd had to. Then I thought I'd give them to the sisters, as payment for taking Julie. That way it wouldn't be charity."

"Julie's lucky to have you," I said.

"No one is lucky to have me," he said. "Haven't you figured that out yet?"

"I am," I said. "I'm lucky."

"Miranda," he said, but I hushed him with a kiss.

July 3

Dad and Matt went into town today for our food. As far as I know, this is the first they've talked since before the trip to the convent.

After they left, Alex came over. "I was wondering if you wanted to go house hunting," he asked me.

We got on the bikes and began riding. I led us in a new direction, and we prowled through a couple of houses, not finding much but not expecting to, either. We worked in silence, staying in the same rooms, but never touching.

"Miranda, I've been thinking," Alex said at last.

"You think too much," I said.

He grabbed me. Or maybe I grabbed him. It's a little hazy. All I know is we were in each other's arms, sharing a long, hard, hungry kiss.

"No," he said, inching away. "This isn't right."

"You're thinking again," I said, pulling him back for another kiss. He wanted me as much as I wanted him.

"Come with us," he said. "Julie and me. We'll be a family."

"What about the monastery?" I asked.

"That was a dream," he said. "Like the safe town. Like the convent. But you're real, Miranda. You and Julie and the world we've been handed. We can make it work. I know we can."

"That's what I want, too," I said.

Alex hugged me. "You won't regret it," he said. "We'll find a priest in Pittsburgh and get married there. I'll get housing for you and Julie while I work in the coal mines. You won't go hungry. I swear you won't."

"Married?" I said. "By a priest? Couldn't we just exchange vows right now?"

"No," Alex said. "We can't keep on like this. It's a sin. Either we get married in the eyes of God and the Church or we stop now."

I reached out to him and grasped his hand. "I'm sorry," I said. "I can't say yes, I'll marry you, and leave everybody I love behind. I love you and I want you, but I'm not ready for that yet. I don't think it's what you want, not really."

"You have no idea what I want," Alex said.

"So tell me," I said. "What do you want, Alex? To be with me? To be a Franciscan? Make me understand what you want."

He stood there so silent I could hear his heart beat. "I want to be good," he said softly. "But I don't know how."

"Oh, Alex," I said, longing to hold him and knowing he'd resist if I tried. "None of us know anymore."

He nodded and then he wept, like a little boy who'd asked for the moon and been told he could never have it.

July 4

I used to love the Fourth of July. Hot weather. Fireworks.

Today was gloomy and 50 degrees.

The guys celebrated the day by chopping firewood. Mom made her regular inspection of our food supplies. Gabriel, I suppose, cried, and Lisa most likely hovered around him.

Syl doesn't eat breakfast. She says she never did and she doesn't see any point starting now. This, of course, drives Mom crazy, but good mother-in-law that she is, she keeps her opinion about breakfast being the most important meal of the day to herself.

So when everyone was busy and Syl was hiding in Matt's bedroom, I went up to talk with her. Which I've hardly done since I've come back, and which, frankly, I wouldn't want to do except there was something I had to ask her.

I knocked on the door and told Syl it was me and she said to come in. She was lying on the sofa-bed mattress, covered with blankets even though the electric heater was going full blast.

"I'm never warm enough," she said. "Except in the sunroom with the woodstove."

"You could come downstairs," I pointed out.

"I will later," she said.

I looked at her and thought about how she'd let Horton out to die, and then I told myself not to think about that, because there was a chance Syl knew something that could help Alex and Julie. "There was something you said once," I began. "About truck drivers."

"What about them?" she asked, propping herself up with her elbow.

"You said they stopped sometimes when they were going to safe towns," I said. "And picked people up."

"Girls," Syl said. "They never stopped for guys. And they never did on the way <u>to</u> safe towns. The trucks would be filled with supplies then. On the way back they might stop for a girl."

"Did they ever stop for you?" I asked.

"What business is that of yours?" she said.

"No," I said. "You don't understand. I was wondering if one of them told you where he'd come from, where the safe town was. That's all."

"No," Syl said. "They knew better than to talk. They could lose their jobs if they told anyone where the safe towns are located."

"Okay," I said. "I'm sorry if I bothered you."

"Sit down," she said. "I hate the way you're standing there, glaring at me."

"I'm not glaring," I said, but I did as she said and sat on the mattress by her side.

"It doesn't matter where any of the safe towns are," Syl said. "None of us could get in. We're not important enough. They're for politicians, people like that."

Syl and Lisa have gotten pretty close. If Dad had told Lisa about the passes, Lisa would have told Syl. Dad must have kept that knowledge to himself, figuring it would upset Lisa. I had to be careful I didn't let Syl know why I was asking.

"It's stupid," I said. "I thought maybe because Mom is a writer, we could get in. That's all. I remembered you mentioned them, so I thought I'd ask if you knew where one is. But you don't, and I'm sorry I bothered you."

For the first time since I've known her, Syl looked uncomfortable. "Look," she said. "There are things I've told Matt and things I haven't, but the only reason I haven't is because he hates hearing about them. All right? I'm not ashamed of anything I did. I'm alive and I'm here because of what I did. Matt knows that. He accepts that. But he doesn't like the details."

"I won't tell Matt," I said. "I swear."

"Scout's honor?" Syl asked, and then she laughed. "All right. I believe you. It doesn't matter, anyway. I was in an evac camp. This was, I don't know, maybe a year ago. Pretty early on. The camps have guards, military police, young guys mostly. And one of them had gotten his hands on some bottles of vodka, so he and his buddies decided to party. Which they did with some of us girls. We left the camp and broke into an empty house and had a good time." She paused. "It was important to keep the guards happy. If one of them liked you, you might get extra food or a blanket."

I understood why Matt didn't want to hear any of this. And I started to understand why Alex and Carlos were so desperate to protect Julie.

"There were lots of girls at the camp," Syl continued. "The guards had their pick, so you did whatever they asked and you tried to make them feel important, like they were the star quarterback and you were head cheerleader."

"Matt isn't like that," I said.

"No," Syl said. "Matt isn't anything like that. Neither is Hal or Charlie or Alex. The guards wouldn't have been like that, either, probably, if things hadn't changed. But things did change, so they were full of themselves, and if you wanted some extra food, you acted like they were the greatest people on Earth. They loved reminding you how powerful they were.

"We were all a little bit drunk that night, and they started bragging about how many people they'd killed.

Then they started talking about the first time they'd killed someone. And one of the guys said the first time he'd killed people was when he'd been assigned to clear out a college to make it a safe town. It was funny, he said, because it was Sexton University and he'd applied there and been rejected, and there he was, shooting professors who were resisting. I said I hope he got the dean of admissions, and he laughed."

"How can you remember the name," I asked, "if you were drunk?"

"I wasn't that drunk," Syl said. "And I was still trying out different names, so I thought about Anne Sexton, only Anne is pretty dull and you can't call yourself Sex. So I went with Sylvia Plath instead. I like her more anyway."

I had no idea who she was talking about but it didn't matter. "Did the guard say where it was?" I asked. "Sexton University?"

Syl shook her head. "He'd said too much as it was," she said. "The next day I heard the girls who'd been at the party were being rounded up and put in a holding pen. I left before they found me."

"But if you knew the name, couldn't you have found it?" I asked.

"I didn't care where it was," she said. "I was trying to make my way east to see if any of my family was still alive. Which they weren't."

"You have family now," I said.

"That's what Matt tells me," she said.

There was nothing I could say to that, except to ask Syl not to tell anyone I'd been asking. I didn't want Mom to find out, I said. Syl agreed.

And now I'm in my closet, writing all this down, trying

to figure out how to find out where Sexton University is and what to do if I can find out.

I have no idea how many colleges there are in the United States, or how many there were, because for all I know now there aren't any. But Dad used to work at Denning College, so I figured there was at least a chance he'd heard of Sexton University and might know where it was.

The only problem was I'd have to give him an explanation why I was asking. It's not like I could say, "Well, I'm thinking about applying there next year because I've always wanted to go to a school named for Anne Sexton, whoever she is."

I have a feeling he'd believe me more if I said I always wanted to go to a school that had Sex in its name, but it doesn't matter. Maybe there are still colleges out there, but unless they're biking distance from Howell, PA, I won't reach it in time for orientation.

I'd have to come up with a different reason why I wanted to know, and there wasn't one. It's not like I could say it came up in conversation or in a game of Name the Most Obscure University. And Dad can always tell when I'm lying.

I figured he could break me down in two steps, if it took that long.

Most likely Mom's heard of Anne Sexton, but that doesn't mean she's heard of Sexton University. And she could break me down in one step without even trying.

Back in the time when life was easy, the Internet would have told me what I needed to know. The great thing about the Internet was it didn't care why you were asking.

But even though we have electricity more often than not, we don't have phone, or cable, or Internet. Maybe they do in safe towns, but I don't live in one.

I tried to remember how people found things out before the Internet existed. They had to have questions, after all, and they couldn't always ask their parents. Or teachers. Or librarians.

Librarians! Librarians always know how to find out things. That was their job even before the Internet.

There was only one problem: The Howell library closed months ago.

But that didn't mean all its books were gone. Maybe there was a book that listed all the universities in the country. And if the library ever did have a book like that, it was probably still there, because who would have stolen it?

The next question was whether I should go to the library and see if I could find the book and get Sexton University's address. If I don't, I won't have to tell Alex. But if I do go, it's specifically to tell him, because why else would I want to know where Sexton University was located, except to fantasize about going to a school that had Sex in its name?

If I told Alex, he would leave. It wouldn't matter how far away it was. He'd wait until he was sure Julie was up to the trip, and then they'd take off and I'd never see either one of them again, unless I went with them, which apparently would require the approval not just of Mom and Dad but the eyes of God and the Church.

But how could I not tell him? And how could I be certain Syl wouldn't let something slip during Bible studies with Lisa and Charlie? Alex would hear about Sexton University, and he and Julie would leave, but he'd leave hating me.

If we were never going to see each other again, I wanted him to at least feel bad about it.

So I biked to town. I lied to Mom, saying I was going to Dad's to play with the baby, and Mom didn't try to break me. I guess some lies are more believable than others. My bike was in the garage, but she didn't notice when I got it, or if she did, she didn't run out to demand an explanation. Nobody else did, either. I biked the four miles to town all on my own.

I don't like going to town. It's a reminder of everything that isn't anymore. It was never a big town, but there were places to eat and to shop and to hang out. And now it's dead, except for City Hall, open on Mondays to hand out food. For as long as that lasts.

As I biked to the library I thought about having to break one of the windows to get in. That seemed horribly immoral, as bad as breaking a window of a church. But lucky for me, someone else didn't feel that way, because the window was already broken. I let myself in.

It was filthy. I don't know why that surprised me, since we scrub frantically to keep the soot manageable and there was no one at the library to do that. But there was something about the library being so cold, dark, and dirty that broke my heart. It felt like losing Horton again.

I didn't cry, though. There's enough to cry about without shedding tears over a building. Besides, if a miracle happened and Mom went to Dad's and found I wasn't there, I'd be grounded for life, which I pretty much am anyway, but this time it would be official.

I walked over to the reference section. Most of the books were still there. Of course most of the books had nothing to do with colleges. I had to dust off the covers of a lot of no longer useful books before I found what I'd been looking for: <u>The American College Guide</u>.

I almost didn't pick it up. I told myself I could pretend I hadn't seen it and bike back home before anyone noticed I was gone and forget all about it, and Alex and Julie would stay with us. At least Jon and Julie would be happy. Didn't I owe it to Jon to keep Julie from going? And Dad and Lisa? And Charlie? And if Jon was miserable, then Mom would be miserable, and if she was miserable, she'd make Syl miserable, and that would make Matt miserable. And everyone would make me miserable.

Ignorance is bliss.

I picked up the book.

The colleges were listed in alphabetical order.

Sexton University was located in McKinley, Tennessee. It had a student enrollment of 5,500 and was best known for its agricultural and veterinary programs.

There's something about succeeding, even at a job you don't like, that makes you push harder. I tore out the page about Sexton University, then located a road atlas. There were five pages devoted to Tennessee, and I ripped them all out. Alex would have to find the state on his own, but once he got there, he could follow the map to McKinley.

Then, because I was all alone in a library and had already destroyed two books, I found my way to the poetry section, located an anthology of contemporary American poetry, and took it for Syl. I might even give it to her someday.

I stopped in at Dad's on my way home. Gabriel was yelling his little baby head off.

"He's teething," Lisa said, like he needed an excuse to scream.

Alex, Jon, and Julie were in the parlor. Alex was giving them a world history lesson. Alex probably felt history still mattered. Julie believed Alex still mattered, and Jon believed Julie still mattered. Or maybe all three of them were actually interested.

I could have interrupted, told Alex then and there about the safe town in McKinley, Tennessee, waved good-bye as he and Julie left us forever, consoled the broken-hearted, consoled my own broken heart.

Instead I gave Alex a quick nod, returned my bike to our garage, and came up to my bedroom closet to write all this down. I'm spending so much time in here, I'm thinking about putting up curtains.

Alex told me to trust in tomorrow. Well, maybe tomorrow I'll know what to do.

July 7

I still haven't decided.

Instead of thinking, I scrubbed the house so clean that if decorating magazines still existed, our house would be the cover

Chapter 16

July 8

I didn't sleep well last night, and when I did, I had the same dream over and over, that I was alone in the house, which was our house but didn't look like our house. It was sparkling and new and I couldn't get over how beautiful it was, but every room I entered was empty. The more I had the dream, the more I knew the house was empty because everybody had died and I was the only person left alive.

After a while I gave up trying to sleep.

I thought about my choices. They seemed pretty simple at first. Either I told Alex or I didn't tell Alex.

Then it got more complicated. I could tell Alex now or I could tell Alex next week. Or I could decide whether or not I'd tell him next week. Or next month. Or next year. Just because I didn't tell him now didn't mean I'd never tell him.

Of course when you can't be really sure you'll be alive a year from now, postponing decisions is the same as making decisions.

That got me back to either I told Alex or I didn't tell Alex. Because it would take him and Julie months to get to Tennessee, and winter comes early these days. Like by the end of August. If I delayed telling him until then, he and Julie would set off anyway and have a lot harder time making it to Tennessee.

For all my talk about choices, I really didn't have any. I'd tell Alex where the safe town was, and I'd tell him right away. He and Julie would stay through Monday. Two days from now.

They'd already stayed much longer than Alex had intended. If the convent had still been open, they'd already have been gone for more than a week. My fantasy that Alex would have stayed with me was just that, a fantasy. He'd made a deal with God. Julie in the convent, Alex in the monastery. And Miranda? Miranda was just another dream.

So I'd tell him. I'd hand him his walking papers.

Nothing lasts except fear, hunger, and darkness. Five weeks ago I wouldn't have been able to imagine what I would feel loving, truly loving, a boy. I'd had feelings. I'd had fantasies. But nothing like what I've felt for the past five weeks. It would have been like picturing a color you've never seen.

Five weeks. Maybe I'll live five more years, or five more weeks, or only five more days. But I've been given the gift of those five weeks, and I shouldn't be greedy for more.

Once I accepted that, it was a matter of waiting until morning. I'm pretty sure I fell back asleep, but the dreams were gone.

I walked over to Dad's after breakfast. Alex and Julie were in the parlor praying. I thought, I have the answer to their prayers, but of course I don't know what their prayers are.

When they finished, I let them know I was there. "I need to talk to you," I said to Alex, but there was still a part of me that thought I didn't have to tell him.

He waited for me.

"Outside," I said. "Let's go for a walk."

I didn't give Alex a chance to ask any questions. If I hesitated, I might not have gone through with it. We weren't ten feet from the house before I handed him the sheets of paper. "Syl says there's a safe town there," I said. "At Sexton University."

Alex stared at the pages. "Has she seen it?" he asked.

"No," I said. "She heard about it from someone who was there when they turned it into one. She didn't know where it was and I lied about why I asked. I went to town, to the library. This is what I found."

Alex read the write-up of Sexton. Then he reached over and kissed me. "We'll go tomorrow," he said.

"It's Saturday," I said. "Wait until Tuesday."

"I hate waiting," he said. "If we wait much longer, Julie won't make it."

"It's just a cough," I said.

"There's no such thing as just a cough," he said.

I held him and we kissed again.

"You'll come with us," he said. There was no question in his voice, just the assurance that I would.

"Alex, I don't know," I said.

"No," he said. "You have to. Now that it's real, that Julie has a place to go, I can make plans for us."

"I'm not a Catholic," I said. "I can't convert for you."

"I'm not asking you to," he said. "I don't love you for what you believe. I love you in spite of what you believe."

"I believe in family," I said. "And so do you."

He nodded. "I thought the passes were the only thing I had of value. But you're what I value. I'll give Lisa two of the passes, for her and Gabriel. Julie can live with them in the safe town. Hal and you and I will live outside of town. Charlie, too, if he wants. They're bound to need workers, people to farm and clean and keep the town running. Miranda, we can do it."

I thought about it as much as I could think with Alex's body so close to mine. I knew the journey would be hard, but it would be harder a month from now, a year from now, whenever the food ran out and we'd have to leave here. And I wouldn't have Alex.

If I left now, Mom would still have Jon and Matt and Syl. She couldn't object if I went with Dad. Even if she did object, she couldn't stop me.

"Yes," I said. "Oh, Alex, yes."

July 9

It was one thing to tell Alex that I would go with him. It was a whole other thing to tell Mom.

I knew I had to. I couldn't vanish. I'd asked Alex to hold off telling Dad and Lisa until today, but once they knew, they'd come over to talk about plans.

It would be even worse if Julie told Jon and Jon told Mom before I had.

But it was Sunday, and Mom politely declined when Syl asked if she wanted to join them for their prayer service. I declined just as politely. Mom and I stood at the door and watched as Syl and Matt and Jon walked over to Dad's. I was alone now with Mom. I had no choice.

"There's something I have to tell you," I said.

I could see Mom calculate how bad it was going to be. But she didn't say anything, just gestured for me to sit by her side.

"Alex has some papers," I said. "Three passes into a safe town."

"What's a safe town?" Mom asked.

"They're towns that still work," I said. "The government set them up. They have electricity, I guess. Hospitals, schools. They're for important people to live in. People with connections."

"How did Alex get the passes?" she asked. "Does his family have connections?"

"What difference does it make?" I said. "He has them."

"It makes a lot of difference," Mom said. "Because the next thing you're going to tell me is you're going off with him and Julie and the three of you will be fine and happy and I shouldn't worry because you'll be in a safe town, whatever that is. But if Alex stole the passes or worse, then I want to know."

"I don't know how he got them," I said. "But I know Alex. He would never have stolen them."

"All right," Mom said. "Somehow these passes fell into his lap. It's a miracle. Why hasn't he taken Julie there already? What was all the business about the convent if there's this lovely safe town waiting for them?"

"He didn't know where one was," I said. "They keep them hidden. I found out for him."

"And how did you find out?" Mom asked.

"That doesn't matter," I said. "I found out. I told him. He and Julie and I will be leaving day after tomorrow. We're going to spend the rest of our lives together. Mom, he's giving up everything for me."

"You're the one who's giving everything up," Mom said. "You're giving up your home, your family."

"No," I said. "That's what you don't understand, Mom. Alex is giving two of the passes to Lisa, for her and Gabriel. He'll let Julie live with them, and he and Dad and I will live together nearby. That's what he's giving up, Mom. Those passes are worth a lot. Alex could trade them for whatever he wants. But what he wants is me."

"And where is this paradise on Earth?" Mom asked. "Where you'll live just outside someplace with hospitals and schools."

"Tennessee," I said. "Sexton University, in McKinley, Tennessee. Alex says we're sure to get work there. You can't stop me, Mom, any more than you could stop Matt from falling in love. I'm going. I'll be with Dad. I'll be all right."

"You're not doing this to be with your father," Mom said. "At least be honest about that."

"I'm more honest than you ever were," I said. "When you kept me from going with Dad last summer."

"I had to make that decision for you," Mom said. "You weren't old enough to decide for yourself."

"I'm old enough now," I said. "And I've decided."

"Does your father know?" Mom asked.

"Alex is telling him today," I said.

"Well, he'll be happy," Mom said. "A safe place for Lisa and the baby. Will Charlie go with you?"

"I don't know," I said. "I hope so."

"I hope so, too," Mom said. "Because you're going to need all the help you can get, Miranda, when this blows up. You think you're grown up but you're not. You have no idea what love is. What you feel for Alex, it's pity and desire, not love. Not the kind of love two people build a life on."

"Maybe that's what love is now," I said. "Pity. Desire. Maybe I'm one of the lucky ones because I still have feelings. I don't know. I just know I can't bear the thought of losing Alex. This is my chance, maybe my only chance, to love somebody. I can't worry about what we'll build a life on. We have today. If we're lucky, we'll have tomorrow."

"What if you don't stay in Tennessee?" Mom asked. "How will I know where you are?"

"We'll let Alex's brother know," I said. "Carlos Morales. He's in the Marines, stationed in Texas. Alex can give you all his information."

"There's nothing I can say to change your mind?" she asked. "You have no doubts?"

I had a thousand doubts, a million doubts. "I love Alex," I said. "He loves me. I'm going with him."

"But not until Tuesday," Mom said. "If you do change your mind, it will be all right. Alex will understand and so will your father. Promise me you'll think about it between now and then. I love you, Miranda, and I want what's best for you. Think about what you'll be giving up if you go. Think about it hard."

"I have thought about it," I said. "And I promise you I'll think about it more. But, Mom, I'm going. I know what I'll be giving up if I go. But I also know what I'll be giving up if I stay."

Mom took my hand. "This wasn't how things were supposed to be," she said. "You should be in high school, your future ahead of you. Not this."

"It wasn't supposed to be this way for Alex, either," I said. "Or Matt. Or Jon. You have to fight for happiness, Mom. Maybe it didn't used to be that way, but it is now. I'm not going to settle for sadness. That's not what you want for me, not really."

"I want to protect you," Mom said. "I want to know you're safe, that you'll be all right."

"Just love me," I said. "Love me and let me go."

Chapter 17

July 10

I thought I knew what fear was. I thought, For the past year I've lived every day afraid; I must understand fear.

I understood nothing.

Last night was horrible. Matt yelled at me, told me that Alex wasn't good enough for me, that I was disloyal and stupid. Then he and Syl got into a screaming match in their room, so loud we could all hear it downstairs.

Jon didn't yell, at least not at me. He and Mom had a huge fight. He wanted to go with us and Mom wouldn't let him. It was so bad she sent me over to Dad's to bring him back to tell Jon he'd be better off staying home.

Even Charlie got in the act. He came over to talk things out with me.

"I'm glad you're going with us," he said. "It makes Hal so happy, and Hal's the best friend I've ever had. But don't count too much on Alex. He's a great boy, Miranda, a wonderful boy, but that's what he is, a boy. A boy who's been given so much responsibility, he thinks he must be a man."

That was last night. And awful as it was, I'd give up everything to go back to it.

Matt and Dad went out this morning to chop wood

and spend their last day together. Syl hid in her room; Jon, in his. Mom and I cleaned downstairs, carefully staying in different rooms as we dusted and scrubbed.

Alex and Julie came over around ten. "Julie would like to make the food run with Jon," Alex said. "Is that all right with you, Mrs. Evans?"

Mom nodded. She went to the staircase and hollered to Jon to come down. He did, each step taking longer than the step before.

"Julie wants to go to town with you," Mom said. "For the food run. All right?"

Jon shrugged.

Julie took that for a yes. "Let's go," she said. Jon followed as she left the house.

"I'd like to go out with Miranda if you don't mind, Mrs. Evans," Alex said. "I'd like to look for bikes or maybe even a car."

"It looks like it might rain," Mom said.

"She'll be fine," Alex said. "I'll look out for her."

"I'll get my jacket," I said. I ran to the closet and got it, giving Mom a peck on the cheek when I returned. "Mom, don't worry. I won't melt."

"All right," Mom said. "I won't worry."

When we got outside, I realized I wouldn't need my jacket. It was very muggy and close to 70 degrees. There was the smell of thunderstorms in the air. I hoped tomorrow would be better. It would be easier for Mom if I didn't leave under stormy skies.

"We need more bikes," Alex said. "You and I can share one to start out with, and one for Julie and Lisa and Gabriel to share, and one each for Charlie and Hal. I figure we can take one bike from your family, so we'll need three more."

"We only have four bikes," I said. "Those are for Mom and Matt and Syl and Jon."

"Your mother won't need one," Alex said. "She never leaves the house."

"She will someday," I said. "When she has to."

"She'll get a bike then," Alex said. "In the meantime you'll need a bike a lot more than she does."

I wanted to ask Alex if we were doing the right thing, but I knew asking him meant I thought we weren't. He must have sensed what I was feeling because he grabbed me and we kissed.

"I want you so much," he said, and then he laughed. "I used to think I wanted things, school, success, food. That was nothing compared to how much I want you."

"You have me," I said.

"I don't believe it," he said, so I kissed him to prove it. And when I did, my million doubts flew away.

"Come on," he said, taking my hand. "Let's see what we can find."

We hiked over to the Seven Pines development, a mile or so away. We stopped more often than I could count, to kiss, to hold each other, to marvel that we really existed. I had lied to Mom. I did melt, over and over again.

It took an hour of searching and hugging and kissing before we found two bikes. "Let's ride them back," I suggested. "And go out again to look some more."

"Good idea," Alex said, kissing me again. "We'll look for two bikes so your mother can keep yours."

We began the short ride back to my house. We rode side by side, but even so Alex felt too far away from me. I thought, I'm choosing to spend the rest of my life with this boy and I hardly know him. But I wasn't scared anymore, just excited and impatient for the next part of my life to begin.

We'd gotten back to Howell Bridge Road, maybe a quarter mile from home, when the wind picked up, howling so hard it knocked me off my bike. Alex got off his bike to help me up, but I pulled him down instead, and we kissed.

What a dumb word that is, "kiss." I've kissed my grandparents, my brothers, my friends, my teddy bears. I've kissed other boys.

This kiss wasn't that. This kiss was two bodies desperately wanting to become one.

"Do you still want to marry me?" I asked him. "In the eyes of God and the Church?"

"Does that mean you will?" he asked.

I nodded. We held on to each other, loved each other, for what should have been the rest of our lives.

But then hail started to fall, little pellets of ice at first, more and more of them, growing in size and danger.

"We've got to get home," Alex said as he pulled me up from the road and helped me get on my bike.

It's been a year since I've seen blue sky, and I thought I knew every different gradation of gray, but the sky had a new and terrifying tone, almost a greenish tint. We rode frantically down the hill, both of us falling as our wheels hit ice. Thunder was growing louder and closer to flashes of lightning.

And then I saw the twister. I couldn't tell how far away it was, just that it was moving fast toward us, toward our home.

I yelled to Alex, who looked as I gestured. We rode even faster then, trying to outrace death. But as we reached my house, he didn't turn off onto the driveway. Instead he yelled something at me and kept on biking, faster than I knew he could, faster than I knew anybody could.

In a flash I understood everything. He was biking toward Julie and Jon, to warn them, to save them. And he'd shouted to me to get his missal.

I had only seconds to decide. Do I go back home, warn Mom and Syl, and ride out the tornado in the cellar with them, or do I go to Dad's, warn Lisa and Charlie, and do the one thing Alex had asked of me?

I turned away from home, rode to Dad's, jumped off my bike, and pounded frantically on their back door.

Charlie opened it.

"Tornado!" I screamed. "Go to the cellar!"

I didn't stay in the kitchen long enough to make sure he understood, that he warned Lisa and led her and the baby to safety. I trusted him to do that, as Alex trusted me.

Instead I ran to the parlor and looked frantically for the missal. I went through a pile of textbooks, but it wasn't there. I felt all the furniture, to see if it was stuffed under cushions, but it didn't seem to be. I got on the floor, searching under the chairs and sofas. I have no idea how long I looked, maybe a minute, maybe more. But then I caught a glimpse of something in his neatly folded pile of clothes. I flung the clothes until I found the missal.

I raced back toward the kitchen, but I could tell from the terrifying sound, the way the house was beginning to shake, that there wasn't enough time to get to the cellar. Instead I ran into the little storage closet under the stairwell, clutching the missal tightly, as though it could keep me from harm.

When we were kids, we were forbidden to go in that closet. It was the perfect size to hide in, and we'd always been tempted. But now I was grown up, and the closet was too small for me to stand. I curled up in a ball, making myself as small as possible, so the tornado couldn't find me.

All around me I could sense the house collapsing, and I felt like a sparrow being sucked into an airplane engine. The sound was ungodly. But the stairwell held, and the tornado passed, and I was still alive.

I pushed against the stairwell door, but it wouldn't open. I pushed harder, shoving my shoulder against it, but nothing happened. I twisted my torso so my entire chest faced the door, and I rammed my body into the door, pushing, pushing, pushing, but the door stayed shut. There was too much debris piled against it.

I was stuck in the closet, in a tiny space under the staircase. I'd survived the tornado, but now I was buried alive. If no one found me, I'd suffocate.

"Help!" I screamed. "Help!"

"Miranda? Where are you? Are you all right?"

The voice was muffled, as though it was a long way away. Then I realized it was Charlie, calling to me from the cellar.

"I'm in the stairwell closet," I yelled. "I can't get the door open. Are you all right? Lisa? The baby?"

"We're fine," Charlie shouted. "Keep still, Miranda. Don't talk anymore. I'll be there in a minute."

I shook from relief. Charlie would save me. Death would be cheated, one more time.

But Charlie didn't come. I heard thuds from the cellar and a noise I couldn't identify, and then Lisa screamed.

I knew yelling would use up needed air, but I couldn't help myself. "What happened?" I shouted. "Lisa?"

Lisa didn't answer. She just screamed, "No! Charlie, no!"

"Charlie!" I shouted. "Charlie, answer me!"

But there was no answer, just the sound of Lisa and Gabriel wailing as though they'd lost their best friend.

I was too stunned to cry. Something had happened. I couldn't be sure what, but whatever it was, Charlie hadn't been able to get the cellar door open. He and Lisa and Gabriel were as trapped as I was. They had more room, so they wouldn't suffocate, but unless someone came and got us out, they would die, just as I would, only their deaths would take longer.

Assuming Charlie hadn't already died.

It was then, only then, that I realized everybody might have died. I hadn't warned Mom or Syl. Mom could have been in the sunroom, Syl in her bedroom, when the tornado struck. Matt and Dad were outside chopping wood. And there was no way of knowing where Jon and Julie were, if Alex had gotten to them in time, and if it would have made any difference if he had.

Before I'd shook from relief. Now my body spasmed in terror and grief.

"Lisa! Lisa, are you all right?"

"Daddy!" I screamed. "Daddy, help me!"

"Miranda?" Dad called. "I can hear you, but I don't know where you are."

"In the stairwell closet," I said. "Daddy, get me out. Lisa and Charlie are in the cellar. Something happened to Charlie."

"Miranda, it'll be all right," Dad said. "I'm in the hallway. There's a pile of rubble blocking the door. I'll get Matt. We'll dig you out. Lisa, can you hear me?"

"Hal!" Lisa yelled. "Hal! It's Charlie. I think he's dead!"

"Lisa, I can't get to you," Dad said. "There's too much debris. I'm going to get Matt and we'll dig Miranda out first, and then we'll get you. All right, darling? Is Gabriel all right?"

"Please." Lisa sobbed. "Get us out, Hal, please."

"We will, darling," Dad said. "You'll be out before you know it. But first we'll get Miranda so she can help us. Miranda, relax if you can. You'll be out in no time."

"Is Mom all right?" I cried. "Daddy?"

"She's fine," Dad said. "So's Syl. We'll be back in a minute. Hold on, Miranda. Just a few more minutes."

I hadn't heard him come in, because of Lisa and Gabriel crying. But I could hear him leave, and the sound of his moving away from me left me even more shaken.

I told myself to calm down. Dad and Matt would get me out and I'd be fine. Mom and Syl had survived. Lisa might be wrong about Charlie. Alex and Jon and Julie had to be all right. They just had to be. We all did. We'd survived worse, I told myself. We'd get through this together.

I realized then how tightly I was grasping Alex's missal, and I thought, I can't let Matt see this. If Matt knew I'd gone for the missal instead of warning Mom and Syl, he would never forgive me.

I knew there could only be one reason why Alex had told me to get it. The passes to the safe town had to be there.

I was in complete darkness, and I didn't have one of my flashlight pens with me. I held the missal upside down, and an envelope fell out.

I felt it. There were certainly papers in it, and something else, something like tiny buttons.

They were pills, I realized. The sleeping pills Alex had told me about. Pills to allow Julie to sleep through her death.

I slid the envelope under my shirt and tucked the missal into the corner of the closet. Matt would never know. I'd give the envelope to Alex, and we'd go off together just as we'd planned. Dad and Lisa and the baby were fine. Julie would be secure in the safe town, and when she was, Alex could throw the pills away. He and I would make our life together. We'd have our tomorrows.

I could hear them then, Dad and Matt and Syl. When I heard Syl's voice, I knew Mom really was all right and I would be also.

"There's a lot of debris here," Dad said. "Miranda, we'll get you out, but it's going to take a few minutes. Just let us know you're okay, and then don't worry about it."

"I'm fine, Dad," I said, crying and laughing. "Take your time."

Dad made a sound I decided was laughter. I listened as he, Matt, and Syl worked together, clearing a pathway to the door. In the background I could hear Lisa crying and Dad calling out to her, telling her everything would be all right.

I felt the envelope against my chest. I told myself Alex was alive, that I'd give him the envelope, and if he had ever needed proof of my love, he never would again.

I don't know how long it took before I could hear Dad pull the door open. A few minutes maybe, or forever. I felt him before I could see him. Dark as it was in the hallway, my eyes still had to adjust to the dim light. But it didn't matter. Dad grasped me and pulled me out.

"You have to be careful, honey," he said. "There's garbage all around, broken glass. Hold on to me, and we'll get you outside."

I followed him blindly, stumbling over the remains of Mrs. Nesbitt's house, my second home. Slowly I realized there was no house left. It had collapsed all around me, only the staircase keeping me from being crushed to death.

After we made it outside away from the rubble, I held on to Dad and let his strength pass to me. Then I hugged Matt and Syl. Nothing that had been said last night mattered. Nothing mattered anymore except that they were alive.

"Jon?" I asked. "Julie? Alex?"

Dad shook his head. "We don't know where they are," he said. "We thought Alex was with you."

"He went to warn Jon and Julie," I said. "But Mom's all right? You said she's all right."

"I'll take you to her," Syl said. "Come, Miranda, you'll see she's fine."

"Come back as soon as you can," Matt said. "We've got to work on getting Lisa out."

"I know," Syl said. "We'll be back in a few minutes." She put her arm around my shoulders and led me toward home.

Within seconds I was standing in the sunroom, in Mom's arms. She held me so tightly I wasn't sure I could ever move away. I wasn't sure I ever wanted to. I know she was crying, but that was all right, too.

"Miranda, we need you to help clear out the rubble," Syl said. "You too, Laura. Come on."

"No," Mom said. "I'll wait for Jon here. He'll expect to find me here."

"He'll find us," Syl said. "You can't use him as an excuse, Laura. Lisa's life depends on you."

"If Mom wants to stay here, let her," I said.

"Stop protecting her, Miranda," Syl said. "Laura, you

talk all the time about how the baby is the most important thing. Well, prove it, and come with us."

"I don't know if I can," Mom said. "I know it's crazy, but I'm so afraid if I leave this house, everything will collapse. I feel like I'm the only person holding things together."

"Everything has collapsed," Syl said. "You've done a sucky job holding things together, Laura." She grabbed Mom's arm and literally pulled her out of the sunroom. "See," she said. "The world came to an end while you've been hiding. Now move!"

I stood absolutely still. But then Mom began running toward Mrs. Nesbitt's, toward what had been Mrs. Nesbitt's but was now nothing but a mountain of rubble. Syl and I followed her. I can't be sure, but I think Syl was smiling.

The debris around the cellar door was much higher than what Dad and I had climbed over. It was taller than we were. And it wasn't like you could take a piece from the bottom and work your way upward.

"Miranda, get the ladder from the garage," Matt said.

I ran to the garage, glad to have a job I could handle. The garage looked completely untouched, but when I walked out with the ladder, I looked at our house. There was a tree limb lying across the roof, and I could see windows had blown out and part of the roof was missing.

Even so, we were the lucky ones.

I walked back with the ladder. Matt placed it against the rubble mountain.

"I'll climb up," Syl said. "Miranda, are you up to it?"

I nodded. We climbed the ladder until we were on top of the heap and began throwing what we could as far away from the house as possible.

"Shouldn't one of us go look for the others?" I asked. "What if they need us?"

"They probably do," Syl said. "But we don't know where they are, and we do know where Lisa and the baby are. We have to take care of them and hope that the others find their way back home."

I knew she was right, but I hated hearing her say it. Being outside, surrounded by mountains of debris, made me understand for the first time how devastating this tornado had been. Mrs. Nesbitt's house had taken the brunt of it, but there was no way of knowing how things were farther downhill, closer to town. I began to shake again.

Syl grabbed my arm and squeezed it tight. "Don't think," she said. "Just work."

There was room for three, and Mom climbed up also. She didn't say anything, just worked alongside, being careful, as we all were, to toss the shingles and roofing as far as possible from where we thought the cellar door was. The mound felt solid beneath us, which was both a relief and frightening. We weren't about to fall through, I knew, but it was going to take a very long time to remove enough of it to make a difference.

I don't know how long we worked, throwing things down, while Matt carefully removed what he could from the outer rim of the pile. Dad worked on the side of the house, by one of the tiny cellar windows, clearing it out, so we could talk with Lisa and get things to her until we could get her out.

The hail had stopped and the thunderstorm had moved away. We could still see flashes of lightning in the distance, but it took several seconds before we heard the thunder. It was still raining, though, and it was hard not to slide as we pushed things off. Matt kept yelling at us to be careful, to Syl mostly because she took the greatest risks, but it didn't matter. Whatever happened happened. We had to get Lisa and the baby out of the cellar before the cellar roof collapsed. Which we all knew could happen at any time.

It was Syl who spotted Jon first. From her vantage point on the mound of rubble she could see the road and Jon running up it toward us.

"It's Jon!" she cried. "He's all right."

Mom climbed down the ladder so fast she almost fell into Dad's arms. None of us could stop her as she made her way through the fallen tree branches toward him.

"Do you see Alex?" I asked Syl. "Is Julie there?"

"Just Jon," Syl said.

I climbed down the ladder, but Syl stayed where she was and continued to work. Matt and Dad stopped, though, and we followed Mom's path. We watched as she held on to Jon the way she'd held me earlier. Her children had survived.

"Julie," Jon said. "She's hurt. Mom, she's hurt real bad."

"It's all right, son," Dad said. "Show us where she is. We'll bring her back."

"How bad?" Matt asked. "Is she bleeding?"

"I don't know," Jon said. "I don't think so. But she can't move her arms or her legs. And she said she can't feel anything."

Dad and Mom exchanged looks. Only Matt continued to focus on Jon.

"What exactly happened?" he asked. "How was she hurt? Take a deep breath, Jon, and tell us everything you know."

"We saw a twister coming this way," Jon said. "We tried to take cover, but there wasn't time, so we held on to a tree. I thought I had her covered, but the wind picked her up, and she must have landed wrong because she's lying there and she can't move. I didn't want to leave her, but I couldn't carry her up the road all by myself, and our bikes are gone." He looked around. "Everything is gone," he said, and he began to cry.

Mom took him in her arms. "It's all right," she said. "Your father and Matt will get Julie. Our house is still in one piece. We'll take care of her."

"What about Alex?" I asked Jon. "Did you see him?"

Jon shook his head. "It was just Julie and me," he said.

"Come on, son," Dad said. "Matt, go into the house and get some blankets. We'll use them as a stretcher."

Matt ran to our house, and moments later he came out with the blankets.

"Laura, you, Miranda, and Syl keep working," Dad said. "Jon, show us where Julie is. We'll be back in a few minutes."

"Be careful," Mom said.

We watched them make their way down the road. "Mom," I said. "Should they move Julie? What if she has a spinal injury?"

"It sounds like she does," Mom said. "But there are no doctors, no hospitals anymore. Not here. All we can do is make Julie comfortable."

"No, Mom," I said. "No."

"You have to be strong, Miranda," Mom said. "I'm going to work by the window, where your father was. You stay on the ground. Can you do that? Can you work on the rubble down here?"

I nodded, but I could hardly hear what she was saying. Julie was badly hurt and Alex was still missing. Charlie was in the cellar, dead for all we knew. Lisa and Gabriel were trapped, and we had no equipment, nothing but our hands and our will, to get them out.

Syl had told me not to think. I did as she'd said.

It took a few minutes before Syl spotted Jon. I stopped working and raced toward him. Dad and Matt had improvised a stretcher and were carefully carrying Julie.

I didn't dare ask, but I looked straight at Matt, who shook his head almost imperceptibly.

For a horrible instant I thought he meant Julie had died. But then I heard Dad say, "Hold on, sweetie. We're almost there."

"Alex?" Julie asked.

I'd gotten close enough so she could see and hear me. "He's not back yet," I said. "He'll be home soon."

"I can't move," Julie said. "I tried to. I really tried, but I can't. And I feel strange, like my body isn't attached to me anymore. I've never felt like this, not ever."

"It's okay," Dad said, bending over to stroke her forehead. "Your back is hurt, that's all. You'll be up and around in no time."

She looked so small, so young. I kissed her on her cheek. "Alex will be so proud of you," I said. "You're being very brave."

"He'll be mad," she said. "He gets mad at me when I do things he doesn't like."

"He loves you more than anything," I said.

"We'd better get her inside," Dad said. "Where's Laura?"

"Working by the window," I said.

"Get her and send her in," Dad said. "She can watch after Julie while the rest of us work."

I walked rapidly toward Mom, and for the first time I

can ever remember, I cherished the sensation of movement. Hours ago I'd been trapped in the closet, and now I was outside and I could walk and run. Julie had lost that, most likely forever.

Mom seemed reluctant to go indoors. I guess after all those months, she was cherishing the sensation of sky and air and freedom. Dad took her place at the cellar window, and he insisted Jon work by his side. Matt worked on the ground, and I went back to the top of the mound and resumed throwing things down.

It got dark eventually, and Dad sent Jon to the house to get lanterns and flashlights. Hours later they broke through to the cellar window. It had blown out during the storm, but it was too small for Lisa to crawl through.

Still, Dad was able to talk to her, and when she held Gabriel up, he could hold him. Jon was sent back to our house to get food for Lisa.

Dad returned a while later to tell us what he knew.

"Charlie was pushing against the cellar door," he said. "Trying to open it, but of course he couldn't. Lisa isn't sure what happened, because it was so dark, but she thinks he had a heart attack. She heard him make a funny noise, and then he fell down the cellar stairs. She went to him, but she couldn't find a pulse. He probably died instantly."

I thought, Charlie's dead because of me. I told him to go to the cellar. He tried to open the door to rescue me.

I knew that was crazy. If I caused Charlie's death, then I saved Lisa's and Gabriel's lives. If Charlie tried to get out for me, he was also trying for himself and for them. But I still felt the guilt, like the tornado was somehow my fault, and Julie was hurt because of me, and Alex missing.

"We're not telling Lisa about Julie or Alex," Dad said, much more softly. "I told Jon not to say anything. I told her Julie's back in the house and Alex has gone to look for help."

"How long can we keep that up, Dad?" Matt asked.

Dad grabbed him by the arm. "As long as we damn well have to," he said. "Now get back to work."

And we did. I'd be working there still, except Dad decided we should work in shifts, and I was sent back to the house to eat and get some rest and stay with Julie. Mom left as soon as I got here.

Julie's sleeping, but I can't. I'm too scared.

I wish more than anything that it was last night.

Chapter 18

July 11

The rest of my life, I'm going to be living a lie, so I'm writing now to tell what really happened.

No, even that is a lie. It isn't what really happened. It's what I made happen. If I don't admit that here, now, then I'll be lying to myself just as I'll be lying to everyone else every day of my life.

We spent all day working, trying to move the mountain of rubble that was blocking the cellar door and keeping Lisa and Gabriel trapped. We can get Gabriel out through the window, but only Lisa can feed him, so there's no point. She has food and water, and Mom cut up a couple of Matt's flannel shirts, for diapers. Sometimes when he cries, we hear him, and it makes us smile, at least for a moment, at least on the inside.

We hardly talk. The only breaks we take are when we're coughing so hard we have to stop. A few sips of boiled water, and we get back to the job. It's better that we don't talk. There's nothing we could say that wouldn't make us sadder or more afraid.

All the food Jon and Julie got is gone. All the food at Mrs. Nesbitt's is gone. We don't know for sure, but we can't count on more food deliveries from town. We don't know if there is still a town.

The electricity is out, but this time it will never return. Wires are down and there's nobody to repair them. There are two big tree limbs on the front of our house, and part of the roof has caved in. A handful of the windows shattered as well. It's funny. Matt used to worry about us losing the sunroom roof, but that made it through. It's the rest of the house that's collapsing around us.

Dad had put Julie on the sunroom mattress. We took turns going in, checking up on her, making sure the fire was still burning, and eating enough to keep ourselves going, grabbing what sleep we could by Julie's side.

We didn't talk about Julie except once. Mom said she'd taken a pin and stuck Julie's hands and feet with it. She told Julie to close her eyes and let her know when she felt something. Six times Julie hadn't felt anything. Three times she said she thought she felt the pin, but two out of those three times Mom hadn't pricked her.

"I don't understand," Jon said. "What does that mean?"

"It means Julie wants to believe she still has feeling," Syl said. "But believing it and having it are two different things."

"But she'll get well," Jon said. "Won't she?"

"No," Mom said. "She won't, Jon."

"Is she going to die?" he cried.

"Not so loud," Dad said. "We don't want Lisa to hear."

"I don't care about Lisa!" Jon said. "What about Julie? Can't we do something?"

"All we can do is make things as easy for her as possible," Mom said. "You're not a child anymore, Jon. You know what things are like."

None of us had stopped working while we talked about Julie. It was early evening, and the pile was down to four feet, so we stood ground level, stooping to pick up the debris. Our backs and arms were screaming in pain. But we kept flinging shingles and siding and pieces of mangled furniture as far from the cellar door as possible.

"I don't want her to die," Jon said.

"None of us want her to," Dad said. "But we don't want her to suffer, either. At least Charlie died fast. Sometimes I think that's the only thing we can hope for anymore."

"No, Hal," Mom said. "We can still hope for our children, for their future. That's all that matters, their future."

I thought about the future I'd imagined for myself two days before—Lisa, Gabriel, and Julie in a safe place; Dad and Alex and me near enough that we could see them sometimes, know they were being taken care of; having that future Mom wanted for all of us.

It was more than twenty-four hours since I'd seen Alex. A part of me was starting to think he'd never existed, that I'd made up a boy I'd given my heart to because he wouldn't accept anything less from me.

But I knew he was real because I missed him so much, and because his sister was lying helpless in the sunroom and we were talking about her death.

Alex had thought about her death. He'd prepared for it. He'd accepted something I had never had to, that there might come a moment when death was preferable to life and that he bore the responsibility of recognizing that moment and acting on it out of love.

He'd been so concerned about leaving Julie in Dad and Lisa's care because no matter how much they loved her, they weren't family. But when I'd agreed to marry Alex, I'd become Julie's family. That's why Alex had told me to get his missal. He knew he was risking death, biking into the path of the tornado. But he trusted me with the only possessions of value he had, the passes and the pills.

All of that came to me while I worked, every one of those thoughts, those realizations. And once they were in my mind, I thought them over and over again, like the nightmares I'd had, endlessly looping through my mind until I finally accepted the truth. Alex was gone. Julie was my responsibility, no one else's.

I don't know what time it was when Mom told me to go home, to send Matt back, and to get some sleep. All I know is we were working by lamplight then, and the night was so clear you could make out the full moon through the ashen sky.

I stumbled to our house, the darkness and my exhaustion making it almost impossible to walk a straight line. Matt was sleeping and I hated waking him, but we needed every hand we had. He didn't say anything when I shook him awake. All he did was nod and walk away.

I lifted the blankets off Julie to see if she needed changing, but she was dry. I'd hoped she was asleep, but when I saw her eyes were open, I asked if she needed anything.

"No," she said. "Matt gave me some food and water. But I wish Alex was here."

I stroked her face. "Alex loves you," I said. "We love you, Julie. All of us love you."

"I wish I could see Lisa and Gabriel," Julie said. "And Charlie. Charlie always makes me laugh."

"You'll see him soon," I said. "I promise you that."

Julie began to cough, and when she did, her body shook. I lifted her so she was in more of a sitting position and had her rest against my chest until the coughing stopped. There were three pillows on the mattress already, but I asked if she'd like another. She said no.

"You're like the princess and the pea," I said, knowing what was coming but postponing it for another hour, another minute. I remember hoping that Alex would somehow fly in and Julie would be miraculously cured.

But I'd been hoping for miracles for over a year now. Another hour, another minute, was never long enough.

"What's the princess and the pea?" she asked.

"It's a fairy tale," I said. "About how the only way you can tell a true princess is if you put a pea under forty mattresses. If she can feel it, then she's a true princess."

"What a waste of a pea," Julie said.

"When they wrote fairy tales, they didn't know," I said. "They had peas to spare in those days."

Julie giggled.

"Did your mother tell you fairy tales?" I asked. "When you were little?"

"No," Julie said. "But she liked it when we told her about the saints. We learned about them in school and we'd tell her what we'd learned. Joan of Arc was my favorite. I wrote a report about her once."

"I didn't know she was a saint," I said. "I guess I never thought about her being one."

"She was," Julie said. "She's the patron saint of soldiers."

"She's your brother Carlos's patron saint, then," I said.

"Maybe," Julie said. "Maybe the Marines have a different one. Carlos says it's better to be a Marine than a soldier. He'd probably rather have his own patron saint."

"You believe in all that," I said. "You and Alex. In spite of everything you still believe?"

It was dark in the sunroom, just the glow from the woodstove, but even so I could see the look of surprise on Julie's face. "Of course," she said. "I'll see Santa Maria, Madre de Dios, when I'm in heaven."

"What's heaven like?" I asked. "Do you know?"

"No one's hungry there," Julie said. "Or cold or lonely. You can see millions of stars at night, like that painting. And there are gardens. Big vegetable gardens filled with everything. Tomatoes, radishes. String beans. They're my favorites, the string bean plants."

"No flowers?" I said.

"You can have flowers if you want," Julie said. "It's heaven."

She began coughing again, her face contorted, her body in spasms. I held her, comforted her, told her soon she'd be all right.

We could both tell she'd soiled herself. "I'm sorry," she said. "I didn't mean to."

"Don't worry about it," I said. "I'll get a washcloth and clean you and change your clothes."

She began to cry. "Don't leave me," she said. "Please. I made Alex promise he'd never leave me to die alone."

I think that's what she said. But she might have said Alex had promised he'd never leave her to be alone. I can't be sure.

"I'll just be gone for a minute," I said. "Why don't you say a prayer while you're waiting? That's what Alex would want you to do."

I left her praying in Spanish. I walked upstairs to my room, got some fresh clothes, then took a washcloth and towel from the bathroom.

We're not supposed to stay upstairs any longer than we

have to. The roof could cave in anytime. But still I waited for a minute, a second, hoping for that miracle I knew would never happen.

I stopped in the kitchen, wetted the washcloth, then poured Julie a glass of water. Maybe I thought about Alex. I'm not certain. All I remember is opening the envelope, taking out two of the pills, and shaking so hard the water spilled out of the glass.

Julie was quiet when I returned. I pulled off her pants and underpants, cleaned and dried her as best I could, and put on the fresh clothes. Then I lifted her gently, raising her head and back from the pillows she'd been resting on.

"I want you to take these," I said, showing her the pills. "They'll help you stop coughing."

"I can't hold them," she said.

"No, you can't," I said. "Wait a second. I'll put them on a spoon for you." I rested her tenderly on the bed again, went back to the kitchen, and put the pills on a spoon. Then with my left arm, I lifted her again, placing her head in the crook of my arm, and with my right hand I spoon-fed her the pills. When I was sure the spoon was empty, I put the glass of water to her lips and watched as she swallowed.

"Say a prayer and go to sleep," I said. "Think about heaven, Julie, and your dreams will be sweet."

I think she prayed. I think she said thank you. I think I heard her murmur, "brie," and "poppy." I know I kissed her on her forehead and told her she would never be hungry or scared or lonely again.

I remembered a prayer Grandma had taught me. I knelt by Julie's side and put my fingers on her mouth so God would know the prayer was for her, not me.

Now I lay me down to sleep.
I pray the Lord my soul to keep.
If I should die before I wake,
I pray the Lord my soul to take.

When I couldn't deny to myself anymore that she was sleeping, I eased one of the pillows from beneath Julie's head. I held it down for as long as I could, until I could be certain, for her sake, for Alex's, that she was in the healing embrace of her Holy Mother.

I returned the pillow to its place and gently kissed her good-bye.

She didn't wake up.

She never woke up.

July 12

Syl woke me. "I'm sorry," she said. "There's water coming into the cellar. We have no time to waste."

"Julie?" I said.

"She passed while you were sleeping," Syl said. "Freshen up, Miranda, and I'll go tell the others."

My diary was in my hands. I'd fallen asleep in the sunroom and never put it back in my closet.

Syl had pulled one of the blankets over Julie's head. Two days ago Julie'd biked into town with my brother. Now she was just another of the dead.

I went to my room, put the diary in its hiding place, then returned to what had been Mrs. Nesbitt's. We worked continuously, not even stopping to get food for Lisa.

The water was waist high when Lisa and Gabriel crossed the cellar to wait for their rescue at the top of the stairs. The moon had risen by the time Dad could pull the cellar door open. They raced out, away from the house, the rubble piled high on either side of them. One of the mounds collapsed inward, but they were already safe.

Dad told her then about Julie, about Alex. I think Lisa had already guessed it, because she was the one comforting Dad as he stood there weeping.

Chapter 19

July 13

The roof caved in on Mom's bedroom that night. We'd slept in the sunroom together so none of us were hurt.

Matt had carried out Julie's body and rested it on Jon's mattress in the dining room, but it didn't matter. We felt her presence. Charlie's, too. I sensed Mrs. Nesbitt with us, and so many other people I've loved and lost.

Alex came home.

I knew he would. He would never leave Julie to be alone.

"I was lost," he said. "I don't know how that happened. I wasn't that far from here, but the wind tossed me around and I lost all sense of direction. How long have I been gone?"

Three days, we told him.

"I didn't know where I was," he said. "Then this morning I saw the mound of bodies. Most of them were gone. The wind scattered them in the fields, on the road. But there were enough left that I could figure out where I was and find my way back."

I'd gotten up to be by his side, to hold him when he heard Dad's next words. "We have bad news for you, son," Dad said. "Julie passed away. Two nights ago. Charlie died the day before."

I could feel Alex's body shudder.

"She wasn't alone," I said. "We never left her alone. I was with her when she died. She prayed. We talked about your mother, about saints, about heaven. Julie said it was filled with vegetable gardens, with tomatoes and string beans."

He dissolved then. Whatever strength he'd had to get through the storm, to get through the year, melted in a moment. He collapsed onto the floor, sobbing as I've never heard anyone sob.

I knelt beside him, held him, kissed him, but his pain was beyond anything I could say or do. When finally there were no tears left, I led him to the dining room to be with his sister.

It's been hours. He's still in there. The rest of us take turns, going to the flower garden to say good-bye to Horton, to Mrs. Nesbitt's to say good-bye to Charlie. One of us is always by Alex's side, holding his hand, praying with him. Jon stayed the longest, but Jon had his own prayers to say.

I stood in the doorway watching, listening. I heard Dad tell Alex what had happened. I can't be sure Alex understood. He wasn't there when Julie couldn't move, couldn't feel. We were trying to describe a color he's never seen.

Mom doesn't pray, but she knelt by Alex's side, put her arm around his trembling shoulders. "We're going to have to leave in the morning," she said. "We'll start by going west, all of us together. We'll stop when we can find food, people, work. If we have to, we'll turn south. It won't be easy to leave. It will be harder for me than anything I've ever done. It will be harder for you, because you'll be leaving Julie behind. But we can't stay here. The house is falling in on us. It's collapsing, Alex, but you have to believe the world is still there. The house is gone, Howell may be gone, but there's a world to live in, a world that needs us. We're family, Alex. You're part of us. You always will be, just as Julie was, as Charlie was, as Mrs. Nesbitt was."

Four days ago Mom was afraid if she took a step outside, her world would collapse and all she loved would be lost.

Now Mom is the one telling all of us that we have to leave.

Alex will come with us. He may not want to, but he will because I'll tell him to and he loves me. And he'll have to tell Carlos what happened. Carlos lost a sister, too.

There'll come a moment, a day from now, a week from now, when Alex will ask me about the missal. Did I find it? Do I have it? That's what's on endless loop in my mind now: Alex asking me about the missal, the envelope, the passes, the pills.

I could lie to him. I could tell him I never found it. We'll have our life together, not the one with Julie, but some kind of life based on family and love and lies.

Or I could tell Alex part of the truth. I could hand him the envelope and ask him to let Lisa and Gabriel and Jon use the passes. They were the people Julie loved the best outside of him and Carlos. Julie would want to know they were safe. She would offer them that gift if she could.

Alex would notice right away, though, that there are only four pills. "I took two the night after Julie died," I'd say. "I'd lost Charlie, Julie, my home. I thought I'd lost you. I had to sleep but I couldn't, so I took two of the pills."

He'd believe me at first. He'd want to believe me, and maybe it wouldn't have sunk in yet what Julie was like, that the moment he'd dreaded had come, when her death was preferable to life.

But I know Alex, in the way you can know someone

only by loving him. He'll ask me again and again about Julie's last moments. How did she look? What did she say? Was she at peace with God?

Eventually I'll let something slip. Or I'll get so tired of the questions, I'll shout the truth at him. In my anger I'll want him to know.

Or maybe I'll want him to know, need him to know, because unless he forgives me, I will never forgive myself.

Of course he may never forgive me. Not for killing Julie. He would have done that himself. But for not trusting that he would return, that he would live up to his responsibilities, that he would face his own damnation.

I wouldn't tell him until after Jon and Lisa and Gabriel were safe. I can hold out until then. We'll go together as a family, crossing Pennsylvania, making our way south to Tennessee. It will take months, but we're strong, we're all strong, and we have reason to live. If Alex asks me to marry him between here and McKinley, I'll say no. I'll say it's too soon after Julie's death, that neither of us is ready, that I'll marry him only after he's been to Texas and told Carlos what happened.

Maybe Alex will have guessed by then what happened and be relieved when I finally admit it. Maybe his love for me is deep enough to forgive me, to accept me. But if it isn't or if he can't, I'll have made sure he's free to seek solace in his Church. I have so little to give him, but I can give him that.

This is the last time I'll write in my diaries. I'm choosing not to burn them. They're witness to my story, to all our stories. If I burn them, it's like denying that Mom ever lived or Jon or Matt or Syl. Dad and Lisa. Gabriel. Mrs. Nesbitt. Charlie.

Julie.

Alex.

I can't deny them their stories just to protect mine. So when we go in the morning, I'll leave the diaries behind. I'll never write in one again. My story is told. Let someone else write the next one.

There've been times in my life when I thought I knew everything worth knowing, the sweetness of a robin's song, the brilliance of a field of dandelions, the exhilaration of gliding across the ice on a clear winter's day.

This past year I grew to know hunger, grief, darkness, fear. I began to understand how lonely you can feel even when all you want is to be alone.

Then the rain came. And I learned so much more.

From Syl came lessons of survival. From Gabriel, the message that despair can give birth to hope.

Charlie showed me friendship and family can be one and the same.

Without Julie I wouldn't have remembered that the darkest sky is filled with stars, that the sun casts its warmth on the coldest day.

"Miranda?"

That's Alex's voice, Alex calling to me. I'll put the diary away now, hiding it with all my others. I'll go to him, stand with him, hold his hand as he takes his first steps toward life.

He taught me to trust in tomorrow.

"Yes, Alex," I say. "I'm coming."

SUSAN BETH PFEFFER's first two apocalyptic novels, *Life As We Knew It* and *The Dead & The Gone,* were widely praised by reviewers as action-packed, thrilling, and utterly terrifying. *Life As We Knew It* received numerous starred reviews and honors and was nominated for many state awards. Ms. Pfeffer lives in Middletown, New York.

www.LifeAsWeKnewIt.com